MURDERING SAVAGES

MURDERING SAVAGES

A WESTERN DOUBLE

UZZIAH MOUNTAIN MAN
BOOK TWO

J.J. BONHAM

WOLFPACK
PUBLISHING
EST 2013

Murdering Savages: A Western Double
Paperback Edition
Copyright © 2025 (As Revised) by J.J. Bonham

Wolfpack Publishing
1707 E. Diana Street
Tampa, FL 33610

www.wolfpackpublishing.com

Paperback ISBN 979-8-89567-807-7
Ebook ISBN 979-8-89567-806-0

MURDERING SAVAGES

MURDERING SAVAGES

1

Uzziah and Immanuel were sitting outside the three cabins which Immanuel had built, those long years ago. It was early spring and they were sitting by a fire with a coffee pot sitting on it, and they each had an empty cup in their hands. Obviously, they were waiting for the pot to percolate.

Articles were flying out of one of the cabins. Chairs, a table, bear blankets, packs, extra traps, you name it, it was flying out the door. There was muffled yelling inside that particular cabin, but it was impossible to hear what was being said.

"Too bad she's got the coffee, we could have a cup," Uzziah said, chuckling.

"How long will she keep this up?" Immanuel asked.

"Got me. What'd ya say to her?" Uzziah asked, looking at his partner as he ducked a flying trap.

"Not much."

"Well, ya musta said somethin'!"

"I made a comment," Immanuel said.

"A comment!" It was Leah, and she was at the door

of the cabin where things kept flying from. "A comment! Tell him, tell him what ya said!" She was livid, her face flushed, and the anger pulsated off of her.

"I mentioned something 'bout the new curtains," Immanuel said sheepishly.

"Something! Something!" she yelled and went back in and started ripping the curtains off the windows and throwing them out toward the fire. Immanuel grabbed one set and pulled it from the flames.

"This here material belonged to the one whose name I can no longer say," Immanuel said as he straightened the torn and scorched cloth out.

"So damn what!" Leah was at the door again.

"So, it wasn't your'n to use, and you overstepped your place here...again!" Immanuel said, getting up and walking toward Leah, who retreated back into the cabin and continued on her tear. The noise was deafening.

"I didn't realize there was that much stuff in that cabin," Uzziah commented.

"There wasn't 'til she packed it in there."

A fire poker flew out, spinning over and over in its length, barely missing Immanuel's head.

"You gotta do something," he said to Uzziah.

"Me?"

"You're the one who went off with her to bury her pa, and ya come back like she's yer bride."

"I did no such thing!"

"Yes, ya did! And ever since then, she has acted as if these were her cabins, and everything in them belongs to her!"

"All I wanted to do was make them more like a home!" Leah screamed at them through the window where curtains had been torn down.

"How much like home does it feel, Uzziah, huh? Feel like ya wanna hang out here at our home? Ya gotta do something! You brought her here with an understanding which I was not a part of, and in one short winter," he said, pointing at the cabin, "she has turned into the harridan of the Rockies!"

"I heard that," Leah said sticking her head out the door. "What's that mean, hair-a-den? Huh? What's it mean, Uzziah? He just keeps using fancy words so I won't be able to tell how he really feels!"

Immanuel went for her and was faster than she imagined he could be. He grabbed her and brought her over by the fire.

"Sit down and shut the hell up!" he said, brandishing his fist at her.

"You see, Uzziah, you see how he treats me!?"

"Now, ya listen to me. That bolt of material that you took and cut up and made yer curtains, and whatever else ya made, that there cloth belonged to my Injun wife."

"Ya mean ya was something besides the half-man ya are now?"

Uzziah got up more to defend his friend than to help her. "Settle down, sweetheart," Uzziah said as he patted her on the head. She tore his hand off her head and bit it.

"Damn! What has gotten into you, woman?!" Uzziah asked, literally licking his wound.

"Neither you nor him have been into me, what are you two fellas? Are ya strange in the man way?"

"I thought ya was doing her?" Immanuel said.

"Well, I thought ya was," Uzziah said.

"Nah, didn't want to impose myself."

"And each time she came from your cabin, I thought, well, I guess she's his," Uzziah said, smiling.

"Well, that's what I thought, that she was your'n. She stayed in your cabin more nights."

"But I didn't touch her!" Uzziah protested.

"Neither one of ya did, what the hell is wrong with ya two!?"

Immanuel and Uzziah started laughing and pointing at one another. The longer they laughed, the more hysterical it got.

"What's the joke? Ain't I desirable?"

That put both the mountain men over the edge, and they laughed so hard that they had to hold their bellies and roll in the dirt.

Leah came over and kicked Uzziah where he was rolling, and he grunted but continued to laugh. Then she went for Immanuel and he grabbed her leg and brought her down before her foot could connect with him.

He got on top of her and held her flailing arms down.

"What the hell is wrong with you, woman?"

"I've been wanting a blanket hornpipe, and you two ain't up to it!" she confessed.

"Ya mean yer this angry because we didn't make bread and butter with ya!?" Immanuel asked, and he started laughing again.

Leah kicked up out of the position that Immanuel had her in, and when she cleared him, she kicked him and ran away into the woods.

Immanuel sat holding his side, either from all the laughter or from being kicked. Didn't matter, it hurt, and he hadn't had this much fun all winter.

"You shoulda done yer duty," he chuckled, looking at Uzziah.

"She ain't my bride."

"Nor mine. She has to go, and ya gotta tell her that," Immanuel said as he stood up and brushed off his deerskins. "We ain't gonna get anything done 'til she's gone. Figure out how yer gonna do it, when I get back, we'll pack and take her back to Vrain Trading Post," he said as he grabbed his saddle and got it on his horse's back. He picked up some of the traps she had thrown during her fit and placed them into his saddle bags.

"I'll be back in a while," he said as he rode off.

Uzziah watched him leave and then looked to where Leah had run into the woods. She was returning from her retreat, and the look on her face was not welcoming.

"Ya through throwing yer tantrum?" Uzziah asked her.

She looked at him and he prepared for her to attack him, then she broke down into tears.

Uzziah had been around his ma when she was pregnant, all those times when it wasn't him she was pregnant with. He hadn't remembered the first few after he was born, but he had a solid recollection of how crazy she would get when she was pregnant. He wondered how Leah could be pregnant if she hadn't slept with either of them.

"Ya sure ya didn't have a brush with Immanuel?"

"Why would ya ask that? Are ya jealous?"

"Yer acting like my ma when she had a bun in the oven with my brothers and sisters," he said simply.

"Well, ya can't have a bun if there ain't been no kneading and no yeast! Ya dumb son of a bitch!"

Uzziah stood up and walked toward her. His expression was none too nice.

"Ya can call me or Immanuel whichever ya like, but when it gets down to callin' my ma names, well, girl, ya just earned yerself a ticket outta these mountains. Immanuel and I are takin' ya back to the trading post at Vrain."

She looked at him, scowled, and scowled some more.

"I ain't gonna go there. There's too much history there, and the men that come in there treat me like a whore," she said.

"Well, do ya charge 'em?" Uzziah asked, knowing how the one whose name he couldn't say had charged everybody except him and Immanuel.

"You two are the most insulting men I've ever met, and I ain't gonna go back there!" she said and retreated into the cabin.

———

Uzziah had been playing with the tumblers, the pigeons, over the winter, and just to hear from some people who weren't around, he'd sent a few messages to Oscar and Ophelia Blanchard, and each time, they would send a message back to them. At one point, Oscar had mentioned that his little brother had shown up out of the blue right before winter started and he had plans to stay.

He wrote out a quick note letting the couple know they were headed their way. He didn't bother to tell them he was bringing hell-on-wheels Leah with them, but if she didn't want to go back to Jean Baptiste and the Vrain Trading Post, he couldn't think of anywhere else to take her. After all, she was a woman and probably needed another woman around. Regardless of what he and Immanuel had thought during the winter with her going back and forth from one cabin to the next, neither man had consummated a relationship with her. He wasn't sure what Ophelia and Oscar would think, but having two babies on her hands, Ophelia could probably use some help.

When Immanuel got back, he and Uzziah had a talk.

"Did ya tell her?"

"Yeah, I let her have it!" Uzziah said proudly.

"You lying chicken-shit varmint!" Leah screamed from the cabin.

"Good job. I see she's settled back down," Immanuel said, using irony, which he loved.

"Yeah, but she ain't gonna go back to the trading post, so I thought of something else."

"What else?" Immanuel wanted to know.

"The Blanchards," Uzziah said, "Ya know his brother showed up, 'member right afore winter set in?" Uzziah said and raised his eyebrows.

Immanuel thought for a moment, then looked toward the coop where there was only one pigeon.

"Ya done sent a message?"

"Yeah, well, figured we couldn't just show with no warning, and all," Uzziah said, looking toward the cabin, which Leah was straightening up, then whispered, "'Pecially since she's all mother bear and all."

"I heard that, bastard!" Leah yelled from the cabin.

"And I thought I had good hearin'!" Uzziah said.

"She agreed?" Immanuel whispered to Uzziah.

"Told her about the young man staying with the Blanchards," Uzziah said, grinning.

"But we don't know hide nor hair of this boy?"

"He can't be that old, or that young, right? I mean, he came all the way to their place," Uzziah said, hoping.

"Seems like a cruel thing to do to the man who saved our bacon, then took Two-Jays off our hands."

Uzziah merely shrugged, then added, "Well, they may not even be up for visitors. We'll wait for the message to get back to us."

———

It was amazing how Leah had changed. Just the idea of being around other people, people who did not know her from the Vrain Trading Post, had picked her spirits up considerably. She came out of the cabin she had destroyed and was trying to put back in order.

"Hey, Immanuel, I owe ya an apology," she said as she wandered over to where he and Uzziah were sitting.

Both men tensed up as if this were some kind of trick.

"Ya'll still worried 'bout me, ain't ya! I really am sorry," she said and actually hung her head in mock shame.

"Well, I'd say that was about right, pretending to be sorry and all," Immanuel wondered what this apology was going to sound like.

"I am sorry, really. Didn't know I was using something which belonged to another woman, even if she were dead. And besides, I figured that every family needs help with chores, and since there's a younger man involved, well..." She paused, and Immanuel could tell that Uzziah had led her on a bit too much. "I can be a better person and realize that between the three of us there never was nothin,' even ifn I wanted there to be."

"Apology accepted, but ya know we never met Oscar's brother, so we're sorta shootin' in the dark here," Immanuel felt like he should at least be that honest with her.

"Well," she said, "it's the first shooting in the dark ya done all winter."

They got the joke and enjoyed it with more laughter, chuckling, really.

"Yeah, but Uzziah said Oscar is a dern good-lookin' man, and so's I figure his brother, well, he might take after the same family traits," she said and started to walk back into the wrecked cabin, whistling a tune which Immanuel wasn't familiar with.

"Hey!" Uzziah said to her, and she turned in the doorway, "We still gotta wait for the message to get back to us."

"Yeah, I know, the pigeon thing," she said and walked back into the cabin and continued cleaning up.

2

The message by tumbler pigeon came back within a couple of days. It still seemed amazing to Uzziah that messages—short ones albeit—could be sent across such long distances, and a bird could deliver them. He thought of the possibilities in society. There might come a day when pigeons would be delivering messages all over the world, who knew?

They started out the next day after the message, and you'd have thought that Leah was going to go see her bridegroom. They honestly had no way of knowing if Oscar's brother was whatever! They simply didn't know.

They were going to take this time to get her settled in, and then they were going back to their cabins where they'd have an almost complete spring season of gathering pelts, and along with the ones they collected in the fall, they would make their way to sell them. They had had a few discussions about where they would sell them. Immanuel was all for going back to the

Rendezvous, but Uzziah hadn't been pleased with the trades they'd made there.

Uzziah had picked up a story about there being a fur trading post in Taos, Nuevo Mexico. He had missed the warmer weather of Virginia and had heard that the weather in Nuevo Mexico was a lot warmer than the Colorado territory.

Leah traveled well, and both mountain men thought there was probably a lot of reasons for that. One, her father had been a trapper and she had traveled extensively with him. Second, she was sure, for some reason, Immanuel thought it was Uzziah's description of Oscar's farm and the brother, who may or may not be good-looking. Regardless, they had little to no trouble with her. In fact, she offered to cook on the trail and they let her. When they were less than a day away from the Blanchards' place, Immanuel took the opportunity to talk with Uzziah while Leah was off taking a bath in a stream that was nearby.

"You really think this will work?" Immanuel asked.

"What's that?" Uzziah asked as he helped himself to a second serving of beans, bacon, and biscuits.

"This fairy tale ya done told Leah about her handsome prince."

"Well, it has worked so far," Uzziah said, referring to the fact that they had had no more trouble with Leah since Uzziah had installed the story of Oscar's brother in her head.

"Yeah, but what if...ya know?"

"I realize the man saved our bacon with Captain Thomson. If he hadn't been there, we'd be fish food still."

"And ya think bringin' this thunderstorm of a woman into their lives is a good way to repay them?"

Uzziah looked at his friend. They had been together for just a bit over two years, and they seemed to know each other fairly well.

"I don't know what's gonna happen, partner, all I do know is, hope is a strong medicine, so let her have her medicine as we ride toward her prince."

They talked no more about it, but when Leah came from the brook where she'd bathed, she smelled good, and they figured she must have put some toilet water on. Or maybe it was the fact that she was finally fairly clean? They couldn't tell.

———

When they rode into the Blanchard's settlement, the first thing they saw was the makings of another cabin. Oscar and his brother must have been building it. It was a good-sized cabin, set back a little way from the original place. Ophelia came out and was all smiles.

"Oh, my," she said as she was carrying Charlie on her hip and their own boy was running up beside her, holding onto her apron strings, "It is so good to see you two. Please get down and come in and have some refreshments."

Leah was looking around for a man, any man.

"You're probably wondering where Oscar and Willet are?"

"Willet, is that his name?" Leah asked.

"Yeah, they went after meat for the table and should be back by dark."

———

They waited and talked of times past. Leah heard the story of how Oscar had killed the man who was posing as a British Dragoon Captain.

"Oh, I think he was a captain in the Dragoons, he wasn't pretending about that, but something happened to him," Uzziah said, circling his index finger around his temple.

"You could say that, something like the Devil, hisself, invading his person. The man had better luck than he ever deserved," Immanuel said, thinking of how he had survived the Dalles rapids in a canoe and come back to almost be the end of him and Uzziah.

It had been dark for almost an hour, then they heard horses come riding in.

"That's them," Ophelia said, and Leah jumped up like she was about to shit herself.

Leah was the first one out of the cabin door, and she left it open for the others. They all gathered out there in the twilight as the two men were cutting the dead deer and one elk, which they'd killed from the back of their horses.

Immanuel could tell which one was Oscar, but he was sure that Leah wouldn't have a clue. She walked up to Oscar, who was one good-looking young man, and spoke to him.

"Are you Willet?" she asked him, then added, "I'm Leah."

"No, I'm Oscar, that there is Willet," Oscar said, pointing at the other rider, who was just about to dismount.

"You're Willet?" Leah asked.

"Yes 'em," he said in a bass voice as he took off his hat and revealed the fact that his hair only extended around his ears and on the very back of his head, otherwise, he was bald as a cue ball. "Pleased to meet ya, ma'am."

Uzziah and Immanuel got busy helping the two men with the meat that they had just delivered, and Immanuel remembered how well Ophelia had made them venison steaks the last time they had been there.

Leah had withdrawn a bit into the company of Ophelia and the two children.

"I thought he was Oscar's little brother, ya know?" Leah sort of whispered to Ophelia.

"No, no, Willet just means he's shorter than their pa, who was named William," Ophelia explained.

Once the men had come back in from hanging the meat in the coolness of the barn. They came in, Oscar kissed his wife, and Willet went immediately to the coffee pot, which was hanging over the slight fire in the fireplace. He poured himself a cup and sat down at the table across from Leah.

"Oh, I am sorry. Would you like a cup?"

"Yes, please," Leah said and smiled like she'd just been crowned Queen of England.

Willet got up, fished up a cup, wiped it out with his shirt tail, poured coffee into it, and set it in front of Leah.

"So, Leah, what are ya doin' in these parts?" he asked her quite frankly.

It must be said here that Willet was not that much older than Oscar, maybe fifteen years, which put him in his mid-forties, which was not a youth. But he had manners and always looked right at you when he talked and could carry on a good conversation when given a chance. Both Uzziah and Immanuel could tell that she, Leah, was not exactly enamored with the man, but they decided they would just see how things rolled out.

Uzziah helped Oscar out with the coop. The pigeons had bred and there were more of them. That took only the better part of one day. Immanuel was busy cleaning up the traps they were going to place when they got back to the mountains. All in all, it looked like Leah and Willet were doing fine, even though he might have been closer to her pa's age than to hers, maybe not?

———

They left and went back to the mountains. The morning they set out it was cool, but the sky promised no rain, and it looked like it all might just burn off. The birds, it seemed all of them, were singing for the mountain men. Uzziah kept trying to see which bird was singing which song, but looking up into the trees, he could barely catch a glimpse of any of them. Oscar had given Uzziah and Immanuel two carrier pigeons, two tumblers, and Uzziah had them on the back of Shadow. Every time a bird sang out, the pigeons tried to answer.

When they got back to the foothills, they both took the requisite number of traps and went their separate ways. Uzziah went south and Immanuel went north, they would meet in the middle.

This trapping of fine beaver pelts went on for the rest of spring. They were getting some fine coats and it didn't seem like the beaver population in the areas they were trapping were lessening any. It did them good to know that there would be beaver for years to come.

Back at camp, after cleaning and scraping the pelts and stretching them out on the tender branches of trees, they sat around the supper fire and had a nip or two from the bonded whiskey Immanuel liked to keep around.

Uzziah would sip the whiskey and bang a few nails on the coop for the pigeons, which Immanuel thought was silly. How could they possibly find their way in the air back to the Blanchards? He simply didn't believe it.

"We got much more of this?" Uzziah asked.

"I ain't saying. Ifn I tell ya there's plenty you'll drink too fast, and if I warn ya we're running low, then you'll sip yer life away. Better to just drink as ya drink, and when it's gone, it's gone."

"Let's take the furs to Taos."

"Nuevo México?"

"Si."

"Oh, I know what you want, you want them warmer climes that yer used to," Immanuel said.

"I want to see something besides the things I've already seen, is there anything wrong with that?"

Immanuel looked at his partner, and he knew it was a good idea. Go south and into Spanish territory so they might be able to get a better price for their furs. The last Rendezvous, they heard word that the fashion in Europe was changing from beaver hats to silk hats. Someone had told them that silk came from worms and that there were worm farms all over the far east, where this new material was coming from.

"No, old son, there's not a thing wrong with that. I ain't never been out Nuevo Mexico way, so why not!"

He raised his glass fruit jar to Uzziah, who raised his, and they toasted on it. That usually meant that what was said was righteous and would be done.

————

They continued gathering fine pelts all spring, and when the summer was in the air, they packed up their pelts, and they had a shite load. Samson was used for most of them, and once again, she would not take a bridle or lead rope, but they knew how she operated. The pelts that were left over, they put on the mule, who needed the lead rope, and complained for the first 100 miles as they made their way south. They figured it was crazy to get into the open plains with all the wealth they were carrying, so they stayed in the foothills where they could both remain hidden and also be able to see who was out on the plains.

It took them nearly two weeks to get into the Sangre de Christos Mountains, then they simply dropped down into Nuevo Mexico and down into Taos. The town had been around since the 17th century and had recently been turned into a fortified plaza and a trading center with the nearby Taos Pueblo, after which the town had taken its name. The correct name for the town was Don Fernando de Taos. There were sixty-three Spanish families living in the Taos valley, and the American mountain men who traded there were under Spanish law.

The plaza was surrounded by shops in which you could buy just about anything you wanted. There was a fur dealer there also. Immanuel and Uzziah saw the sign for the fur trader and they pulled their horses and mule up to the hitching post and tied up. They stood next to their horses and waited on Samson. She always made her grand entrance, and it was no different this time. As she made her way into the plaza, there were shouts of glee and men whistling at her, trying to get the load of furs that was tied to her back. But she resolutely went directly for Uzziah and Immanuel.

"Good girl, good girl," Uzziah said as he patted her on the rump and gave her the last part of an apple he had bought. She had never, it seemed, had an apple, and the saliva that ran from her mouth was a testimony to that.

Meanwhile, Immanuel had gone into the fur trading company and the man who ran the place had come out to look over the furs.

"Jew know," he began in his thick Spanish accent, "that the moda, the fashion, she has become changed."

"Yeah, we heard. Something about silk," Immanuel said and waited for the bad news.

"Si, si, seda, silk as you say, now all hats are made like this," he said, shaking his head and showing off his silk top hat as he looked at all the beaver pelts.

This seemed like a preamble to a really low price, and Immanuel was setting himself getting ready for the low ball on the pelts.

"How much?" Uzziah finally asked.

"It's mucho pelts."

"How much?" Immanuel was getting impatient.

"Si, si, and five years ago, Mother of God, one years ago, the price would be so much better."

"Are ya gonna tell us or cheat us?" Immanuel asked.

The Spanish man in charge of the fur company looked at Immanuel. He was used to dealing with these mountain men, and he was, by Dios, tired of it. He wanted to say something derogatory, but he also knew that these men had short fuses, well, some of them, and it was impossible to tell who was who.

He wrote something on a piece of paper in a little notebook he pulled from his shirt pocket and showed it to Immanuel, who whirled away and walked down the boardwalk a piece, trying to control his temper.

"Let me see," Uzziah said, coming over beside the man with the notebook.

The man gladly showed him his figure written down in the book.

"It's more money than we got right now," Uzziah said to Immanuel.

Immanuel came over and, taking the stub of a pencil from the man, wrote his own figure in the book, then showed it to the man.

His eyes grew big, then he did something he probably shouldn't have done, he laughed.

"*Senor, por favor*," he said and wrote another figure in his book.

Immanuel looked at it, and he laughed and wrote yet another figure in the book. The man looked at it and did not smile.

"You want too much," he finally said.

"You give too little," Immanuel said and wrote another figure in the book.

The man looked at that figure and rocked back and forth.

"I can go there minus this," he said and wrote another figure in the book.

Immanuel showed Uzziah.

"Now, old son, ya gots to member those early mornings standing in that freezing water and all else that we do. Does this seem fair?"

"No, but as the man said, the moda, the fashion, has changed."

"You mean to tell me, 'cause some Johnson-sucking Frenchman decided he wanted silk on his head, we have to pay the price, or rather not get paid the price?"

"That's what it looks like," Uzziah said, smiling at both men.

———

Immanuel split the monies they received right there, on the spot. Uzziah had his coin purse filled and, actually, he was happy. It would have taken him a lot longer with a lot more work to make that kind of money in Virginia and he knew it.

Immanuel, on the other hand, was disgruntled and gave the man who had paid them such a dirty look that Uzziah thought he might pull his weapon and have at the man.

"Will you help unload the pelts?" he asked Immanuel.

"Hell no, there your'n now, and if they ain't off my animals by the time I get out there, they're mine all over again!" he said and started for the door of the trading post.

The man shouted out something urgent in Spanish, and three young boys were out by the horse and unloading the mule and Samson before they arrived at their mounts.

"Guess he thought ya meant it," Uzziah commented.

"I did," was all Immanuel said as he rode the short distance to the cantina on the corner.

Uzziah had seen this before. When Immanuel got mad and was unable to release his anger in an appropriate way, he drank hard and long.

3

Uzziah woke up in an alley. His horse, Shadow, was standing guard over him since he'd passed out there and slid off his back. He was literally standing guard. Two hombres tried to approach the passed-out American and the horse nearly took off one of their ears. The man ran away holding his ear, which was bleeding badly. Uzziah snored on. Every man should have such a horse.

When the flies were buzzing around his mouth, where he'd thrown up what looked like a burrito, and he was tired of swatting them away, he rolled over and was accosted by the sun, which was fully halfway across the alley and shining in his face.

"What the—" he said as he sat up, and some children playing nearby screamed and ran away. They thought he was dead.

Uzziah wiped his mouth off and nearly gagged but held down what was left in his stomach. He stood by holding on to Shadow, and pulled himself up by the stirrup skirt. He staggered there, trying to get his hat back on properly, and was adjusting his belt and pants when a man spoke up.

"Your horse is a champ," the man said with just a touch of a southern accent. Sounded to Uzziah like the man was from Texas, or maybe Florida.

He looked at the man who was dressed poorly and carried a wineskin over his shoulder, and a few other items were stuffed into a cloth bag.

"Yes, yes, he is," Uzziah said.

"Yer from the south," the man said so proudly that you'd have thought the two men were related, and in a way, they were.

"Virginia," was all Uzziah was able to get out.

"Here," said the man as he offered him a drink from his wineskin.

Uzziah looked at it and was about to say *no thanks* when the man took a sip himself and sighed.

"It's awful good. I'm from Florida, and we make good brandy down there," he said and proffered it again.

"What the hell," Uzziah said and took a sip, then when he tasted it, took another longer pull.

Uzziah straightened himself up again and looked at the man.

"I was traveling with another man—"

"Celda," the man said.

"Is that a woman?" Uzziah asked, thinking his partner had hooked himself up.

"No, we wish, then when we all went there, we would be comforted, but not so, my friend, not so. It's the local jail."

"How? Why?"

"I just got in on the end of what was happening,

25

don't know how things got into such a state, but here's what I saw."

He went on to describe how, late in the evening, he'd made his way to the cantina. He liked to sing, and sometimes, when the mariachis were playing, they would accompany him. He sang songs of the south and other songs, and, he told Uzziah, when the crowd was the right crowd, mostly Americans, he made some money that way.

"So, how'd my partner get into the goad?"

"He struck an officer of the Mexican Army and knocked him out," the man said, then added, "and sadly, the man has not awakened since that blow."

"Two questions. Where's the jail, and where's the man who was knocked out?"

———

They went down to the jail and, looking in the back windows of all the cells, he found Immanuel sound asleep and snoring on a wooden cot and covered with a nasty blanket.

"Immanuel! Immanuel!" he yelled, but when the jailer started down the hall toward the cell, he left.

When they arrived at the doctor's, it was up a flight of stairs and over a cantina, not the one he'd gotten into the fight in. Uzziah left the man from Florida, his name was Randy, down the flight of stairs and climbed them by himself. When he opened the door, he was greeted by a woman in Spanish dress, who had a scarf over her head and was weeping. Her children, three of them, ranged in age from three to six, Uzziah imagined.

He was lost as to what to do or what to say, then a

curtain was drawn back and the doctor stepped out. Uzziah could see a man in uniform lying on a table, he was out, that's for sure.

"*Medico, Medico,*" the woman said, still crying and coming right up to the doctor, who took her by the hands.

"*No te preoccupies,*" the doctor said, which seemed to calm the woman down. "El Vivira," he said and went to his desk in the corner of the room. The woman went and sat back down, digging into her bag and giving the little children some candy.

Uzziah walked over to the doctor, who was seated and writing something in what looked like a journal.

"Just a minute," the doctor said when he could feel Uzziah standing there, then he put down the pen and turned in the swivel chair toward him.

"You hurt?"

"No, sir," Uzziah said.

"You got an hombre who's hurt?"

"No, sir."

The doctor just looked at him as if to say, well, what the hell?

"That man in there—"

"Captain Sanchez, yes, what about him?" the doctor asked, but the woman had heard her husband's name and was paying attention to the pair of gringos now.

"Can you step out here for a moment?" Uzziah asked, and he and the doctor stepped out onto the small landing right outside the door.

"What about Captain Sanchez?"

"Will he live?"

The doctor looked down the stairs and Randy smiled.

"What he tell ya?"

"Just that he was here."

"Tell me, what'd yer friend hit the captain with?"

Uzziah motioned for Randy to come up the stairs. He did so.

"What did my partner hit the captain with?"

"His fist."

The doctor looked incredulously at Randy.

"His fist?"

"Yep."

"He must have a hell of a punch then."

"Oh, he does, he does," Uzziah said proudly then realized there was a man fighting for his life in there.

"I don't know. I've seen men die of lesser things and others who come back from greater trauma."

"Better hope he lives," Randy said, "Around here, Americanos get strung up when they kill a member of President General Santa Anna's Army."

"Thanks, Doc, and if I can help in any way, please let me know. Hey"—he thought better of his offer—"give this to the captain's wife," Uzziah said as he handed half of the money he'd made on the pelts to the doctor, then he and Randy went back down the stairs.

———

Back behind the jailhouse, Uzziah could see that Immanuel was at least awake. Sitting on the wooden bunk and holding his head in his hands.

"Immanuel," Uzziah said loud enough for him to hear, but not the jailer.

He looked up with one eye, which was bloodshot and bleary. Recognizing Uzziah he stood, wavered a bit, then staggered to the window.

"Hey, get me outta here," he said in a breath that rivaled the worst breath Uzziah had ever smelled.

"Not that easy," Uzziah said and filled him in on the Mexican captain's condition, his wife, and three kids.

"Why'd I hit him?" he asked, and Randy spoke up.

"He insulted your mother," Randy said.

"Who's this?"

"Randy, Immanuel. Immanuel, Randy."

"What'd he say?"

"Most of it was in Spanish, and we were all surprised ya knew what it meant, but it was something like *Chinga la madre*."

"Well, who the hell hasn't heard that one?" Immanuel asked.

"I haven't," Uzziah admitted.

"He told yer friend there to do something carnal to his mother," Randy explained.

"What'd ya hit him with?" Uzziah asked, just fact-checking.

"My right," he said, pulling up that fist. It was obvious there were several bones broken in it. "Can you get me a doctor down here?"

"Yeah, maybe, I don't know," Uzziah admitted.

"He'll come, but ya'll hafta pay," Randy said.

"Immanuel, how's yer finances?"

Immanuel checked himself and couldn't find his money, none of it.

"I been robbed!" he shouted, and the jailer came back down the hallway.

"*Vamonos!*" the jailer yelled at Randy and Uzziah and made a motion for them to leave.

They left from behind the jail.

"You hungry?" Uzziah asked Randy.

"Yeah, well, singin' fer yer supper should tell ya somethin'," he said.

They walked to the plaza, and there was a restaurant that touted that it served breakfast, Americano.

They went in, and the place wasn't that crowded. They took a seat by the window. There was a nice breeze, and it was warm.

"I love the weather here," Uzziah said.

"Yeah, Mexico got herself a good part of the country," Randy said, then added, "But it does snow in the winter here, ya know that, right?"

"Sure, but when spring comes here, it's really spring."

A waitress came over and looked at Randy.

"He's got money, he'll pay," Randy said, looking at the board over the window in the kitchen that advertised their food.

"I'll have the ham and eggs. Ya got any grits?" Uzziah asked.

"Yes, grits, we have grits," the woman said. He couldn't tell if she was Mexican or not, but she didn't have an accent. Maybe being in the sun down here had turned her brown, who knew?

"Then give me six fried eggs with the yellow still runnin' and a couple slices of ham and grits."

"Tortillas or toast?"

"Toast."

"Give me the same," Randy said and smacked his lips together.

They sat there drinking their coffee, watching the plaza.

"What all do they sell out there?" Uzziah asked.

"Just about anything ya want."

Uzziah shook his head and sipped his coffee.

"Good coffee, huh?"

"Yeah," Randy said as he poured some brandy into his cup, "Better coffee now."

Uzziah watched him take that sip, then placed his cup over by Randy, who did the trick and poured some brandy into his cup.

"Better coffee," Uzziah said after he'd taken a sip.

Then, as they watched, there was a parade of sorts. Men, mostly naked but wearing breechcloths, were walking with a cart filled with heavy stones. Most of the men held cat-o-nine tails and were flagellating themselves. The sounds from the ungreased wheels of the cart were both shrill and annoying. The ones who weren't busy hurting themselves pulled large crosses, the crossbeam on their shoulders.

"What the hell are they doing?" Uzziah asked.

"They are Penitentes."

"Penta-what?"

"They are a group of men of the Catholic Church who punish themselves as their Christ was punished. They believe that through this punishment, they will receive absolution."

Uzziah had gotten up from the table and was standing by the window as they passed by.

"Boy, they're drawing blood with those blows. It's outrageous!"

"That is nothing, my friend. This weekend, when

Easter is celebrated, one of them will be tied to a cross and will suffer the crucifixion of the Christ."

"What? Where do they do this?"

"Just outside of town, to the north. You would have passed the hill where it will be done when you came in."

Uzziah remembered seeing three life-sized crosses when they rode into town but had paid little to no attention to them.

"You mean out there where those three crosses are, they will crucify one of their own? What do they do, draw straws?"

"No, no, it's a great honor to be chosen, and sometimes fights break out about who will receive the honor."

The waitress came over and put the heavy-laden plates down. Six fried eggs to perfection, and big slices of ham, grits, and the extra thick slices of homemade bread. It smelled delicious.

He sat back down and was about to dig in when Randy stopped him.

"Let us pray," Randy said and he held out his hand to Uzziah, who took the man's hand and bowed his head.

"Heavenly Father, we thank you for this unexpected bonus, this fine breakfast, which my friend, Uzziah, has bought me. We give thanks for all yer mercies and blessings. We pray a special prayer for our friend, Immanuel James Jones, who lies in prison suffering. We also pray for the man he hit, that he will not die, and cause our friend to be hung by the neck until dead. In Jesus name, Amen."

Uzziah didn't exactly dig in at that point. He was

curious. The Floridian had prayed a laudable prayer, but how did he know Immanuel's full name? That was a curiosity. Uzziah took a better look at his friend from Florida. He was looking for a coin purse, or something which could hold money. Had Randy robbed Immanuel, and if he had, how would that tell him his name?

"How do ya know Immanuel's Christian name?"

Randy had a fork full of eggy goodness surrounded by grits on his way to his mouth, and he stopped half-way, the yokes dripping back down on the plate.

"Well, funny ya should ask me that. You was fairly wasted when I arrived at the cantina. I joined Immanuel at the bar, he was buying shots of tequila for everybody who wanted one. I believe he and the captain was havin' a shot contest, and it looked a lot like your friend was gonna win. Anyways, somewhere in the conversating me and Immanuel was having, he mentioned his full name, I guess?" he said and delivered that forkful to his mouth.

Uzziah had continued to shovel the great breakfast into his mouth and deliver it straight to his hungry stomach. He put down his fork, and characteristically wiped his mouth with the cloth napkin which had been supplied them at the table. He was sure that what Randy had just told him was a lie, or at least it seemed one. Why would Immanuel, who was so private with his name, mention it to a total stranger? Well, okay, his partner was drunk, and maybe, just maybe, but he doubted it.

A priest walked into the café and begged for food. He was given a bowl with scraps from the plates of others.

"Padre! Padre!" Randy said to the man, who looked up, saw his friend Randy, and carrying his bowl, came over to the table.

"*Por favor?*" he asked as he motioned to one of the empty seats at Uzziah's table.

"Sure, sure," Randy said, "Uzziah, this is Padre Antonio Jose Martinez. Padre, this is my new friend, Uzziah O'Bannon."

There it was again. How did the man who sang for his supper know Uzziah's last name?

"Please to meet ya, Padre," Uzziah said, and he took the bowl from the priest and threw its contents out the window, where dogs devoured it in a growling fight.

"Ma'am, ma'am!" Uzziah motioned as well as spoke to the waitress.

"Yes, sir?"

"Bring the Padre whatever he wants," Uzziah said.

The Padre looked at Uzziah and crossed himself. "I am in the presence of a holy man," he said.

"Absolutely not, I love God and all that, but I ain't holy by any stretch of the imagination."

"Do you know the Bible?" the Padre asked with his heavy Mexcian accent.

"Yeah, sorta," Uzziah said, then added, "Tell the lady what ya want."

"Steak, well done, three scrambled eggs, potatoes, and tortillas," he said without missing a beat. "So, you know the Holy Book?"

"Some."

"Do you remember King David?"

"Sure, he and Goliath had a fight."

"And he defeated the giant because he was a holy

man like you," he said and sipped the coffee the waitress had brought him.

"I've done too many bad things, Padre."

"King David, King of all Israel, coveted a man's wife when he saw her bathing naked on her roof."

"Bathsheba?"

"Yes, and do you remember what he did to her husband, Uriah, a name not unlike yer own?"

"He sent him to the front of the battle where he was killed."

"And why did he do that?"

"To have the woman to himself."

"And she was with child from King David."

"True."

"Right, so he was an adulterer, a murderer, and it says in that same Holy Bible that he had a heart after God's own heart."

"Does it say that, really?"

"Yes, Uzziah, it does, so when I say you are a holy man, all I really mean is you, too, have a heart after God's own heart."

"Huh?" Uzziah grunted as the Padre's steak and eggs showed up. He bowed his head, and Uzziah joined him in the bowing as he prayed in Spanish.

They sat there the rest of the morning, drinking coffee and brandy. The Padre partook also, gladly. Then as the sun had reached its meridian, Uzziah stood up.

"You have things to do?" the Padre asked.

"My friend is in the jail."

"The captain?" the Padre asked.

"Not much happens unnoticed in this town, does it?" Uzziah noted.

"The Padre, he knows everyone and everything."

"So, Santa Anna's captain, your friend was the one to knock him into eternity?"

"Is he dead?" Randy asked the Padre.

"No, but he will die."

"How'd ya know that?"

"Because he is an evil man. His wife is crying in the doctor's office, praying that he will pass into eternity. He beats her and the children every time he comes home drunk, and that is almost every night. Your friend had done us all a favor by knocking this man into the next life where he will be punished for his sins."

"But what will happen to my friend?"

"He will hang, but he will go to heaven for what he has done and not to hell where the captain will suffer for eternity, thanks be to God, the Father," the Padre said and crossed himself again.

"But won't they have a trial?"

"Senor," the Padre said, "you are in a different country. Yes, they will assemble and pound gavels on desks and talk a lot, but the end result will be the same. No matter how much God, the Father, will bless him for killing this man, the authorities here in Taos will hang him, simply because they can."

Uzziah stuck out his hand to shake the hand of the priest.

"Thank you for being so honest about it," Uzziah said.

"Well, if you, or your doomed friend, ever need anything, Randy knows where I stay."

4

Uzziah wondered where he was going to stay that night. First things first, though. He went by the doctor's office. The captain was still alive, but his hands and feet were getting purple, and the doctor said that was the usual sign of the body dying.

When he emerged from the doctor's office, who should be at the bottom of the steps but Randy. He took a good look at the man who had helped him since he awakened in the alley that morning. He had no horse. He was dressed in what many would consider rags. Yes, he had the ubiquitous wineskin around his shoulder, and it always seemed full? As for age, Uzziah would have guessed he was somewhere between 35-45, but that was as close as he could get. His beard, if you could call it that, was a thatch-work of hair, here and there, and some of it was long. His hair was wild and unkempt, and it shone in the sunlight with a reddish color. His legs were bowed a bit, but his chest looked like it belonged to another man—big and barrel-like.

"Are ya follerin' me?" Uzziah asked as he made his way down the steps.

"Well, yeah, I am. Ain't had this much fun in I can't tell ya when," Randy admitted.

"Well, just don't ferget, that fun is at my partner's expense."

"Where ya gonna stay tonight?"

"Ya got a suggestion, I imagine," Uzziah said as they walked south down the main street, past the plaza, and into what could be considered neighborhoods.

"Yeah, I got a house down by the river," Randy said, and Uzziah was about to follow him on down when he remembered Shadow.

"Let me get my horse, I left him tied up outside the café," Uzziah said.

"It's not a good idea to leave any horse unwatched in Taos. He may be gone," Randy warned.

"I ain't worried," Uzziah said. "Ifn somebody wants him, they'll hafta pay a price."

"You gonna sell him?"

"Not that kinda price."

When they rounded the corner back at the plaza, there was a vaquero who had taken the reins off the hitching post and was about to mount Shadow.

"You see, this vaquero is about to steal yer horse!" Randy complained.

The Mexican cowboy had on a big sombrero and a set of two guns slung down low. He pranced around Shadow as the horse was trying to avoid him getting on.

"I wouldn't do that if I was you," Uzziah said to the man loud enough for him to hear.

He held onto the reins and walked toward Uzziah.

"Que?" he said, not smiling as he walked toward Randy and Uzziah.

"He don't speak-a-the-English," Randy said.

"Translate fer me, will ya?"

"El caballo es hus," Randy said and pointed at Uzziah, who held out his hand for the reins.

"No, el caballo es mio!" the vaquero said.

"I got the gist of that. Tell him let me see you ride him if he's your'n."

"Montaio si es tuyo," Randy said to him.

"Si, si," the man said as he swung up quickly without Shadow knowing and mounted the horse.

The two of them stood there, the vaquero and Shadow. Shadow's legs were trembling.

"Si, si, es mio!" the vaquero said.

Quite a crowd had gathered. The entire café had emptied out, people stood with their plates in their hands, eating their food and watching.

"Let's step back," Uzziah said to Randy as he grabbed the little man and pulled him away from the horse.

At that precise moment, Shadow shot into the air like he was a bottle rocket. Once in the air, he sunfished and came back down on straight legs. The head of the vaquero snapped so quickly that his sombrero, which was tied to his head by a stampede string, flew off. There was blood on the vaquero's face, as he had bit through his lower lip, and his bottom teeth were now outside that bleeding lip.

The crowd was cheering him on like he was a rider at a rodeo. At first, the vaquero tightened his grip on the reins and tried to pull Shadow's head up, but the stallion lowered his head between his front legs, arched his back, and kicked violently out several times. A couple of the men standing too close were kicked and sprawled in the dirt behind the horse. A cry went up from the crowd and people with their food outside started moving away and dropping burritos and such. Dogs moved in for the food, and Shadow, seeing the dogs, kicked out at them, sending one rolling in the dust after it cried out in dismay.

The vaquero thought he may be getting a handle on Shadow when Shadow crow-hopped a couple times, and he thought Shadow might be played out.

"This is when it's gonna get bad," Uzziah said and pulled Randy up on the boardwalk.

"Won't he stop?" Randy asked.

"He ain't no hat bender, if that's what ya mean. Without me on his back, he's a total outlaw!"

That was when Shadow went up high in a buck, and the swap ended by coming back down facing the other direction. The vaquero's smile had disappeared and it looked like he was looking for a pickup man to take him off the horse.

In the next minute, Shadow jumped, kicked, rolled, swiveled, pawed, reared, and sunfished. Like the nursery rhyme, he was like the cow who jumped over the moon if there had been a moon out and if someone had been willing to ride that cow!

Finally, in an attempt to get away from the horse, the vaquero simply let go and was flung through a store window, the glass shattering and showering around him as he was sprawled out in the aisle of the mercantile store.

Shadow, sweating like he'd just run a race, stood there. Uzziah whistled for him, and he came over.

Uzziah checked him out to make sure he hadn't been hurt in all the jumping and rolling, then mounted him. A gasp went up from those around as they were sure they were about to see another rough rider. Instead, Uzziah put his arm down, and Randy, grabbing it, pulled himself up behind the big man, and they rode off at a trot.

The crowd gathered couldn't restrain themselves, they applauded, and Uzziah graciously tipped his hat to them.

They rode south of Taos, and fairly soon, Uzziah could see that there was a severe break in the landscape. A small shack was perched right on the edge of the break. Uzziah rode up and looked down. Below him, eight hundred feet below, the Rio Grande roiled and splashed toward the Gulf of Mexico.

"You live here?" he asked.

Randy hopped down off Shadow, "Yeah, the man who used to own the house walked out one morning and stepped over the edge. Some think he committed the suicide, but he was old, I think he just stumbled and fell, but no one wanted the house, they said it was haunted, got it a taint."

"Well, good thing taints don't bother me," Uzziah said, then he turned to Shadow.

"Ya see that drop, right?" he said to the horse, who looked down and did a blowing roller.

"Damn, he's a smart horse," Randy said.

"Yep, ain't stupid, that's fer sure," Uzziah said as he got down, and Shadow walked away from the precipice and started chomping prairie grass.

———

That night, after Uzziah had fixed Randy dinner, in payment for giving him a place to throw his bedroll, a terrible wind came up. The house was shaking and the wind was finding ways into the house. Uzziah got out of bed and, taking Shadow by the mane, guided him into the barn, which was further away from the cleft in the ground that led to death. The wind in the barn was cut off better than it was in the house, so Uzziah went and got his bedroll and laid down in the same stall with his horse. Shadow put his nose down and snorted on Uzziah.

"I love ya, too," Uzziah said, and Shadow snorted again.

———————

Uzziah was an earlier riser than Randy. He looked into the shack and the short man was sound asleep. He had to get back into town. He rode in without eating, thinking of the breakfast he'd had at the café on the plaza.

Tying Shadow up to the railing, he was recognized by several people who had seen the vaquero try and steal his horse the day before. They grinned and made comments in Spanish about the horse, which Uzziah did not understand, but he smiled graciously and went on into the café.

He sat at the same table in the window just to watch the plaza. The same waitress came up and he ordered the same breakfast he'd had the day before. As he was sipping his coffee, he noticed a dark Mexican in a white suit eating at the table in the back. The man, who was tall and thin and had a thin mustache that skirted his upper lip, asked the waitress a question, and after she answered, he took his cup of coffee and walked over to where Uzziah was seated.

"If I am being a nuisance," the man said in perfect English, "please tell me to go away."

"Yer fine, what's up?" Uzziah asked in his friendly Virginian manner.

"I am Luis Pedro Manzello, and I am a lawyer trained back east. Taos is my home. I understand you may have a friend who needs my services?"

"Please sit," Uzziah said.

"Muchas gracias," Luis said and sat down, motioning for the waitress to bring him more coffee.

The sun was slanting nicely into the plaza, and most of the vendors and shop owners were getting ready to open. The mercantile shop had boards across the broken window. Birds, mostly sparrows, were hopping around the plaza, cleaning up and chirping. It was a fantastic morning.

"So, your friend, I took the liberty of finding out his name, Immanuel James Jones. I like the name and would be proud to represent him in the courts."

"How much?" Uzziah asked, "I hates to be so upfront with that, but it's crucial."

"Not much. This isn't the way I make my money. My family is one of the sixty-three Mexican families that have lived in this Taos valley for a hundred years or more. My money is, as they say, family, an old money. My interests are justice and freedom."

"Well, freedom is what my friend needs, that's fer sure," Uzziah said, greeting his ham, eggs, grits, and thick toast with a groan of satisfaction.

"I love to see a hungry man eat, please," Luis said, gesturing toward the plate of food.

"Well, yer about to see one!" Uzziah said as he dug in.

Uzziah ate everything on his plate, then some. About six cups of coffee, and then he ordered a coffee roll that was smothered in sugary sauce.

"So, what can ya do fer my partner?" Uzziah asked.

"I will go and visit him first and see what happened there at the cantina."

"Good luck on that, he was so drunk, he don't remember nothin,'"

"How about you? Were you there?"

"Yes, and no. We were celebrating, and so I had too much to drink, too."

"Let's go to the constables and see what we can get out of them," Luis said, as he insisted on picking up the cost of Uzziah's breakfast.

Luis and Uzziah walked out and Uzziah took the reins. Shadow followed them from the plaza to a couple streets away where the jail was.

"I've only been behind the jail to see my friend, this will be different," Uzziah said.

They walked in, and it was obvious that the Mexican Policia knew Luis and he had earned their respect.

"Senor Manzello, how are you today?"

"Muis bien, gracias," Luis said.

"What can we do for you today?" the guard asked, knowing that Uzziah was probably the reason he was there, and he was obviously a gringo.

Luis handed the guard a piece of paper, and

Uzziah, for the life of him, couldn't remember when and where he had written it down.

The guard looked at the piece of paper, set it down, and then, taking up the ring of keys, walked back to the cells. When he came back, he had Immanuel in hand-cuffs and led him down to a room where he invited the two men to join them.

"You must leave your firearms here," the guard said, and Uzziah unloaded every weapon he had on him, which was two pistols, the Hawken which he still carried around like it was his third arm, a Bowie knife, a derringer, and another weapon, a Reid's *My Friend* which was a 32-caliber knuckleduster, which had no barrel, but fired directly from the revolver chambers and doubled as a bludgeon.

The guard looked at all the weapons on the table and shook his head.

"Well," Uzziah said, "a man don't like to be caught with his drawers down, do he?"

In the room, Immanuel kept looking at the cuffs which encircled his wrist.

"Hey, pard, good to see ya," Uzziah said.

Immanuel stood up, and the two men embraced. Uzziah pounded Immanuel on the back.

"I'm so sorry fer doin' this to you," Immanuel said.

"Ya didn't do anythin' to me," Uzziah said, "This here's Luis—he's a lawyer, and he wants to talk to you."

Immanuel stuck his hand over the table, both hands, actually, since they were cuffed together, and shook his hand.

"You will probably be okay if, and it's a very big *if*, if the captain doesn't die."

"What are the chances of that?" Immanuel asked.

"Your pardner, Uzziah, and I will go to the doctor's office after visiting you and will have a better idea of that."

"Weren't ya there just yesterday?" Immanuel asked, looking at his partner.

"Yeah, but the sawbones was a bit wary of what could happen."

"Even if he doesn't die, the court may want you to spend some time in prison—"

"Fer hittin' a guy!?!"

"No, for putting a captain of the President's Army in a coma."

"Get this, Immanuel, guess who the President of Mexico is, now?"

"Who?"

"President General Antonio Lopez de Santa Anna."

"The bastard who killed the prisoners at the Alamo!?" Immanuel said, standing up, his eyes bulging.

"The same."

"Then, I don't stand a peanut's chance in an elephant's enclosure," Immanuel said and sat back down.

"The law is the law, whether it be in the United States of America or Mexico," Luis said.

"That may be, partner," Immanuel said to the lawyer, but they play kinda loose with the noose down this way, don't they?"

"People have been hanged, but still, you haven't killed anyone," Luis said.

"Say, can I speak to my pardner alone, senor?"

"Sure," Luis said, and he left the room, the guard

was standing right outside the door, and Luis said something to him, and he nodded, then shut the door.

"What's your uptake on what might happen?" Immanuel asked Uzziah.

"I think we gotta prepare for the worst."

"Me, too. So, do ya have an extra gun fer me?"

"Nah, let's go a little slower. There are some things I have to look into, but I think no matter what happens, I will get you outta this hoosegow."

"What's with us and the law?" Immanuel asked, chuckling.

"Seems to be in our path, no matter which way we turn."

"All I did was hit the guy. I ain't no John Morrissey!"

"Maybe ya missed yer calllin'?"

———

The lawyer, Luis, and Uzziah walked from the jail to the doctor's office. They made the stairs and just walked on inside. Uzziah noted that there was a priest with the patient.

"This don't look good," Uzziah said to Luis.

"Well, these rites cannot be given to a dead man, they may just be hedging their bets," Luis said.

Uzziah turned to the doctor, who was sitting at his desk.

"Where's the captain's wife?"

"She couldn't bear to stay and watch the last rites be given, but she'll be back."

Uzziah thought maybe she was home too happy to let anyone see her.

When the priest was finished, he walked out and Uzziah got a good look at him. It was Padre Antonio Jose Martinez, the man he'd fed.

"Padre," Uzziah said, not wanting to ignore the man.

"Ah, Senor Uzziah," the priest said, and they shook hands, and the Padre leaned in close and whispered in Uzziah's ear, "Meet me at the café on the plaza after this, *por favor*."

The doctor watched all this with a certain amount of disinterest. True, people were hurt every day, and he cared for them as best he could. There was no hospital, which was where Captain Sanchez belonged, so he did the best he could with the room he had.

"How can I help you, solicitor?" the doctor asked Luis.

"We need an expert's opinion."

"Okay."

"Will Captain Sanchez live or not?"

The doctor rubbed his unshaven chin with the palm of his calloused hand. To Uzziah, the Doc's hands looked like he had run roughshod with a wild bunch at one time or another.

"You know I can't really say. If I tell you one thing and the other happens, what does that make me? Seriously, like I told your friend here, I've seen men with greater wounds recover and men with lesser wounds die."

"So, what you're telling us is, it's up to God," the lawyer put it.

The doctor looked into the examining room, where the curtain was still drawn back, then at the two men. "Yep."

When they left the doctor's office, Uzziah wanted to talk to the lawyer without the priest being there.

"So, what options do we have at this point?" Uzziah asked.

"We pray the man doesn't die and that the colonel of the man's unit feels generous," Luis said.

"Okay, ifn ya need me, I'll be either at the café or down at Randy's place."

"The short man with the continuous wineskin?"

"Yeah, that's the one."

"You have friends in low places that may come in handy," Luis said.

"What's that supposed to mean?"

"It means sometimes, when the proverbial shite hits the fan, that we, as humans, to save those who are dear to us, must improvise," Luis said, looking directly into Uzziah's eyes. He loved it when someone was that direct.

"You mean—"

"A man of the law, such as myself, would be foolish to spell things out—you understand?"

"Yeah, yeah, I think I do," Uzziah said as he shook Luis's hand.

He watched the lawyer walk off, then headed for the café on the plaza.

It was lunch, and the café was packed. There were a couple of tables out almost in the plaza that were unoccupied. Uzziah took a seat at the one furthest from the front door. He hadn't seen the priest yet but decided he'd have coffee and some lunch. As he was seated there, the waitress who had waited on him every time he'd been there walked up. She handed him a black slate which had lunch written on it in chalk.

"I'll have coffee and the trout. Say, ya haven't seen Padre Martinez, have ya?"

"Yes, he's inside all the way to the front," she said as she walked off.

Uzziah got up and walked into the café. He'd looked there before, but the man wasn't there, now he was. He motioned for the priest to come to him. As soon as the priest left the table, it was occupied.

"Let's eat out here," Uzziah said and the priest followed him to the table away from the door.

"Did you order?" he asked the priest as soon as he'd sat down.

"No, just the coffee for me," he said, and he had carried a cup of black coffee from the table he'd just deserted.

"Ya sure?" Uzziah didn't want to be eating in front of someone who was hungry.

"I ate this morning. I'm fine with one meal a day."

"One meal a day would make a stomach think my throat was cut," Uzziah joked.

The priest smiled but did not laugh.

"So, what did ya wanna talk about?" Uzziah asked the priest.

"The captain," he started in, then lowered his voice, "he will not live."

Uzziah sucked in air between his big teeth and looked up into the trees which surrounded the plaza.

"Ya sure?"

"Certain."

"But the doctor—"

"Will be paid as long as the man lives, but once he's

carried headfirst from the office, his rewards, his payments stop. His interest is not entirely monetary, but ya know," he said.

"What makes ya think he's gonna die?"

"I have seen this before. Sometimes, it only takes a tap from the right person and a man goes under. This is the case with Captain Sanchez."

"What the hell?" Uzziah said and looked around as if there was some other help he needed.

"But God helps those who help themselves," the priest said.

"I've heard that, but what exactly are ya talkin' 'bout?"

"Your friend's name—"

"Immanuel—"

"Yes, it means *God with us.*"

"I know."

"Well, we can't have someone with that name being hung this close to Easter."

"We can't—"

"No."

"Why's that?"

"Because God is barely with us now, what will be his presence once someone with his son's name is strung up like a slaughtered pig?"

"I think I git yer drift, but what ya got in mind?"

"I have a plan," the priest said as the Penitentes walked by, flagellating themselves. The noise from the squeaky cartwheel that followed them irritated both the priest and the mountain man.

"Why don't they oil that wooden wheel?"

"Because no one would know they were coming," the priest said.

"About this plan—"

"We will speak no more of it now, but—and I'm sure—when Captain Sanchez dies, we will have to act swiftly."

"Can I help ya prepare?"

"No, my son," the priest said as he reached across and touched the top of Uzziah's hand, "What needs to be done, I can do. Just be ready when you hear that the captain has died, okay? And don't have anything more to do with that shyster lawyer, Luis."

"Really, why?"

"He pretends he's from an old family, but his fortune died when Spain was kicked out of Mexico. He is hoping for payment from the colonel and will make sure your friend hangs."

"Double dippin', huh? Good to know," Uzziah said as he saw the waitress come from the café with his full plate in her hands.

The waitress brought the trout with its fixings out to Uzziah. There were fried potatoes, a salad, and wild asparagus. The priest looked at the trout and smiled.

"Ya want some?" Uzziah asked him.

"Maybe just a bite," he said as he boned the fish using Uzziah's fork, then held the bones with the sliver of trout flesh still on them.

"Thank you, Father, for this trout's life," he said, then slipped the bones into his mouth and chewed vigorously.

Uzziah must have made a face.

"Most people don't know, all the nutrients are in the bones," the priest said and stood up.

"So," the priest said as he was about to leave, "don't worry. I do have a plan."

5

When he got back to Randy's house by the Rio Grande Gorge, he was surprised that Randy wasn't there. He wasn't used to cooking indoors when he could do the same thing over an open fire outdoors.

He'd stopped at the carniceria and found he and Randy some good steaks. He had tried to get what some call ribeyes, but his Spanish was nearly non-existent, and he'd done the best he could. They were good and marbled, and he hoped they'd be tender. He'd paid more than he wanted to, but when you are staying at someone's house, you have to make exceptions.

The fire needed to be down to embers before he put the steaks on, so he rolled up some corn, still in their silk and husk, into the sides of the fire. Most men liked their steaks bloody and he was counting on that. On the same fire, he had boiled some greens he'd found out in the desert. He thought they would be like dandelion greens but wasn't sure. He looked around in Randy's kitchen and found some vinegar, well, pickles in vinegar, and that was good. He liked greens with vinegar on them, and he'd bought a small bottle of hot sauce at the carniceria. He tasted it by putting a drop on his finger and decided it was just right.

He looked up and, walking from town, he saw Randy. It took him about fifteen minutes to get to the house and Uzziah had already put the steaks on by the time he arrived.

"Wow, that smells great!" Randy said, walking up and sitting on his heels beside the fire. The sun was low, but there was plenty of light left. There was a breeze off the gorge, but it wasn't crazy like the night before.

"Watch these, will ya, just need to be turned over once," Uzziah said as he went into the barn where he'd decided he was going to keep Shadow since he was a bit afraid of the 800-foot drop into the Rio.

He opened a sack of oats he'd bought and poured some into a bucket inside the stall. Shadow put his nose down into the bucket, lifted his nose, and curled back his lips to grin—all teeth—to Uzziah.

"Like those, do ya?" Uzziah asked him.

Shadow snuffled and went to eating. Uzziah came up to the horse, patted him on the withers, and spoke. "You are the greatest horse I've ever owned. And the fastest, which I think might come in handy in the next week or so," he said as he thought about the priest's plans. He was sure it wouldn't hurt any plan to have a swift horse in the mix.

He went back out just about the same time Randy was turning the steaks over.

"Hope ya like yer meat nearly raw," Randy said.

"Absolutely."

They sat out there in the open air and ate their

steaks off tin plates that Randy had brought from his house. Uzziah used his Bowie knife to cut his steak and passed it on to Randy after he'd made his cut. The corn was the best, and Uzziah wished he had real butter to put on it, but that would require a cow, and hell, he was always wanting more than his heavenly Father was providing for him, and he knew that at some point in his life, he was going to have to realize that God gave him what he needed, not what he wanted.

The meat was great, and tender, and the blood which dripped from it would bring his strength back. He wished it was he and Immanuel who were eating together.

"Thinking of yer friend, huh?" Randy asked.

"Yeah, is it that obvious?"

"Well, there was a certain wistfulness in yer eyes."

"The priest has a plan," Uzziah said out of nowhere.

"A plan—fer what?"

"If Captain Sanchez dies."

Randy picked his steak up with his hands and pulled a good portion off into his mouth and chewed.

"I'd be careful."

"What do ya mean?"

"Yer talking about Father Martinez, right?"

"Yeah," Uzziah said, really curious.

"Well, his ideas are sometimes unearthly, if ya know what I mean," Randy said, eating the cob as well as the corn on it.

"Unearthly?"

"Yeah, well, let me give ya an example, okey-doke?"

"Sure."

"There was this gypsy who came through here, and

everybody was saying that their cattle were miscarrying and their crops were failing because this guy was in the area. Ya know, lots of folks think gypsies are aligned with the Devil."

"They do?"

"Yeah, round here they do. Anyway, Father Martinez thought he could help the man by pretending he'd died."

"What?"

"Yeah, well, the fool gypsy was so worried about being strung up that he took this medicine that the priest gave him. It was supposed to slow down his heart so that you couldn't find a pulse. So's the gypsy takes the medicine, and it works. Well, the priest had been called away to someone who was dying in the hills, and when he got back, they had already buried the gypsy."

"Oh no."

"Oh yeah, so he waits till dark and digs the guy up, well he thinks he's still alive—"

"Did he save him?"

"No, he was alive because, once the drug wore off, he dug at the top of his coffin till his fingernails had all been ripped off. His hands were bloody, and the expression on his face when he died from no air, well, I never seen anything like it."

"You were there?"

"Well, yeah, who'd ya think the priest had digging up the body? He ain't exactly a worker at his age, ya know?"

"What'd ya do, then?"

"We put him back in his coffin, and I covered the hole back up. No one was the wiser."

"My God," Uzziah said, almost losing his appetite.

"So, ifn old Martinez wants yer man to swallow some medicine, don't let him do it, okay?"

"Yeah, I won't."

"The priest warned me of a Mexican lawyer—"

"Luis?"

"Yeah, ya know him?"

"Do not hire the man unless ya want yer partner hung, understand?"

"Got it."

Randy cleaned up the dishes since Uzziah had cooked and the two of them slept as they had the night before. Randy in his house, and Uzziah in Shadow's stall. As Uzziah was fallin' asleep, he had a terrible dream.

———

Father Martinez had convinced Uzziah to give the medicine to Immanuel, and it worked. They thought he'd died right there in the jail cell. They took him to the cemetery and buried him six feet under.

"The drug will wear off in two hours. We will dig him up after the funeral, and you supposedly leave town. I will arrange to have the funeral close to dusk, so by the time you get back, you'll be able to dig your partner up without anyone seeing."

Uzziah wasn't sure in the dream why he was doing what he was doing. Hadn't Randy told him the story of the gypsy and what had happened to that poor man?

And yet, Immanuel had gone along with the plan. The captain had died, and the kangaroo court which the Mexicans held was as good as nothing. Luis, the Mexican lawyer, had just about handed the verdict to the jury as he had been told he would. Immanuel was slated to hang for the captain's murder the next morning.

Uzziah used his contact within the café on the plaza to slip the medicine into Immanuel's last meal, and sure enough, he'd keeled over, and the doctor had come in and declared him dead.

The colonel who had been at the trial screamed something about the prisoner cheating death.

Everything was going as it should in the dream. Uzziah had gone to Immanuel's funeral, there wasn't anybody there except himself and the priest. Just like the Padre had said, they did the funeral close to sundown, and within the next two hours, it would be dark, and he could dig his partner up.

He left the cemetery feeling weird about Immanuel being in an air-tight box where he would wake up in a couple of hours. Just the same, he rode over the hills and headed for the Sangre de Christos Mountains. He was about to enter the foothills when he heard the rataplan of horse hooves behind him. It was Mexican troops. What the hell! He spurred Shadow into a run, good luck, no one could catch that horse when he was on the run. As the wind swept past his face, he thought about the fact that he had exactly two hours before Immanuel woke. He outran the Mexican troops but was now at least an hour away from Taos. He'd have to turn back and get back to the cemetery as quickly as possible.

He took a turn and headed back. He was halfway back when, out of nowhere, the Mexican troops came out of the brush and surrounded him. He couldn't be caught, that's all there was to it. He tried to rush the men in front by spurring Shadow, but they fired directly into his horse and himself. He heard the great cry from Shadow, the *squeal that horses make when they are mortally wounded. His own wound was not a concern, but as he looked down on his chest, he could tell that it was mortal. He hoped he could comfort Shadow before he died, and then he woke up.*

———

Uzziah was in a sweat there in Randy's barn. He looked over and there was Shadow as safe as he ever was. He got up immediately and put his arms around the neck of the great horse. He chortled deep in his chest, and tears came to Uzziah's eyes. He would just as soon die than part with this horse. Whatever the plan of the Padre was, they were not going to bury his partner and then leave it up to Uzziah to dig him up. He made up his mind to go see the colonel and see if he could ask for clemency regardless.

He saddled up Shadow, and the ride into Taos was great. The way that horse moved under him, he felt as if he were the one doing the walking, the trotting, the running. He went to the café and had his breakfast, the one he'd had the past two days, why change when something was so wonderful. He asked for extra grits and that made things perfect.

When he finished, he rode down to where the Mexican Army had its outpost. He tied Shadow up to the hitching rail and walked up the seven wooden steps to the porch. Opening the door to the office, he saw a corporal sitting at a desk.

"Qui paso?" the corporal asked.

"*Por favor*, El Colonel?" he said in his best imitation of some sort of Spanish.

The corporal got up and went into the inner office, and he could hear men in there speaking a language he didn't understand. He made up his mind, right there and then, that he would learn Spanish at some point in his life. Maybe he would marry a senorita and she could teach him while they were making love?

His reverie was interrupted when the corporal came back out and held the door open for him.

The colonel looked like a very self-important man. His uniform had been fitted into creases all over his body. His jacket, which hung on a hat tree to the left of where he sat, showed many medals, and it too was pressed to perfection. *So,* thought Uzziah, *I am dealing with a man who likes the rules.*

"How can I help a foreigner in our lands?" the colonel asked.

"Well, my friend Immanuel—"

"Si, si, the bad hombre who put my captain into a coma," the colonel said as he took a cheroot from the top drawer of his desk. He held up an extra one, and Uzziah didn't want to be impolite, so he took it.

The colonel lit his cheroot, then leaning across the desk, lit Uzziah's cigar.

The cigar smelled like a trash pile that had caught on fire. He tried not to inhale, but some of the smoke made it down his throat and he choked, just as if there were hands around his neck. He coughed and coughed until the colonel had to come around the desk and pound him on the back. Finally, he stopped coughing.

"Good cigar," he said.

The colonel laughed so hard that he farted and looked at Uzziah to see if he'd heard the fart, and

Uzziah pretended not to, but the smell which came off the flatulence was worse than the pile of trash on fire.

Uzziah gagged and thought he would start coughing again but managed to control himself.

So far, his visit to the colonel had been interesting, but not one thing had been accomplished. He decided to cut to the chase.

"Can Immanuel get bail?"

"Bail, bail?"

"You know, money to ensure he will show for the trial."

"No, no, since you both are from the America above us, my fear would be that he and you would run and never come back."

"What if I promised ya we wouldn't do that?"

"I would laugh since I do not know you, and as far as it goes, you may be a prolific liar and nothing more."

The colonel was using some pretty fancy words in English, and Uzziah thought he might be dumbing up his English.

"How is the captain?"

"Do I look like a doctor? No. I am the colonel of this Mexican Army outpost and nothing more. If the captain dies, then your friend, what did you say his name was?"

"Immanuel."

"A Holy name for a dangerous man, well, anyway. If Captain Miguel Sanchez departs to meet his maker, we will have a trial, and regardless, he will be found guilty. There's no mercy down this way for killers, and as far as I'm concerned, your friend and yourself are nothing but murderers."

Well, that sort of said it all, didn't it? The colonel

was already planning for the hanging of his friend, and that was that.

When he left the colonel's office and the compound, he saw way in the back, the gallows, which was not a temporary structure, but something which had been built with stone. They were serious about hanging people around this part of Mexico, and building gallows wasn't going to be one of the things that made them linger over any sentence of death.

———

He decided he'd go visit Immanuel and see how his mood was. The jailer wasn't happy to see him, but he let Uzziah into the hallway that led to Immanuel's cell. Of course, he was required to lay all his weapons on the table as he had done when the lawyer and he had visited. He walked back to the last cell on the right, and he guessed that Immanuel recognized his footfalls because he got up and was waiting at the bars when he got down there.

The two men shook hands, and it was good to feel the warmth in his partner's hand.

"How ya be?" Uzziah asked.

"Passable. Anything to relate to what's goin' on?"

"Well, obviously, the captain's still hangin' on, but this Padre Martinez thinks he's gonna die."

"Damn!"

"Yeah, to say the least. Anyways, he's got a plan of sorts."

"Whatcha mean, of sorts?"

"He's got this potion which puts a man in a deep,

deep sleep, and no one, not even the doctor, can feel yer pulse."

"What the hell?!"

"Yeah, I know."

"Well, that just might work."

"He's tried it afore, and the man they buried—"

"Buried!"

"Yeah, well, whatcha think they do with bodies around here?"

"But I'd be underground in a box—"

"I know, I don't like the idea—"

"Don't like it, hell, it won't be yous in that box, it'll be yours truly, and I don't much like tight spots."

"Yeah, but you'd be knocked totally out."

"Fer how long?"

"Two hours."

"I get it, pretty slick. Ya ride away from the funeral, come back and dig me up, right?"

"Yeah, well, that was the plan the last time."

"Whatcha mean the last time?"

"He tried it with this other fella, a gypsy, but was called away to do the last rites fer some guy, and when he dug the body up, the guy had suffocated while he was tryin' to dig his way out of the box."

Immanuel went over and sat down on the cot that was attached to the side of the cell with some angle iron.

"Let me hear plan B."

"The captain lives and ya only have to break out of a Mexican prison?"

"Shit! This ain't lookin' good, Uzziah. I do believe this is the tightest spot we, as partners, have ever been in, wouldn't ya say?"

"No doubt."

Immanuel got up and walked to the bars again. Uzziah was holding onto them, and Immanuel took both his hands and held them.

"Look, partner, I knows yer doin' yer best, I do. Lots of men would have left me here to either swing on my own or whatever. Ya didn't do that."

"Well, what kinda partner would I be then?"

"Yer parents are good people."

"What?"

"Yer parents, they raised ya good, otherwise ya wouldn't be standin' here. Just keep yer head on straight, keep looking around and we'll figure this out."

"Ya think?"

"I know. I have so much faith in you, brother, I really do."

"Time's up!" the guard yelled down the hallway.

The two men actually hugged with the bars between them. Both of them felt good about that.

"See ya," Uzziah said, and Immanuel simply raised up his right paw and held it there.

————

Out of the jail and walking back toward the plaza where everything happened, he racked his brain, trying to think of what to do. The Catholic Church, at one end of the plaza, was being decorated, and there was a lot of activity around it. Uzziah decided he better check in with the man upstairs and see what plans he had.

The inside of the church was cool and restful. Even though they were decorating for Easter, those doing so were quiet and respectful. After all, it was a church.

He looked up along the windows and there he saw something which he'd never seen in a church.

It was a bust of Jesus, but instead of being all calm and looking holy, the man had his head thrown back and his mouth was opened, and it was obvious, he was having himself a good laugh.

Uzziah stood there for the longest time looking at that bust of the laughing Jesus. Wow, why couldn't regular religion like the Methodist Church in the Shenandoah Valley have something like that bust of Jesus laughing. It made him feel, maybe for the first time, the humanness of the only Son of God. It helped him realize that between that laughing bust and the guy hanging at the front of the church, all tortured up and bleeding on the cross, there was a story. For the first time in his life, he had compassion for the Son of God. Not that God's son needed compassion, but seeing him laugh like that, the way Uzziah himself had laughed so many times, made him realize that not only was the Son of God on that cross, but a good man, who could take a joke and laugh at one, was hanging up there. Tears, uncharacteristic of Uzziah, came over him.

"It's amazing, isn't it?" he heard someone say beside him.

It was Padre Martinez.

"Hey, Padre," Uzziah said as he wiped a tear off his cheek.

"I didn't take you for a religious man."

"Well, I don't know what drew me in here, but I can tell ya, that bust up there, well, it tore me up."

"Yes, yes, the laughing Jesus, a portrait that we often don't see, or think about," Padre Martinez said, and the two of them stood there admiring it.

"I saw you were down at the compound. Did you speak to the colonel?"

"Yeah."

"Was he his usual self?"

"You mean could he give a shite?"

"Something like that. And Immanuel?"

"What was ya doin'? Follerin' me?"

"Not really, but this is a small town."

"I told him 'bout yer plan?"

"And?"

"He weren't too happy about yer trial run."

"Yes, that was unfortunate."

"Got other ideas, Padre?"

Martinez looked around the church. It was looking beautiful for Easter Sunday, which was in a few days.

"Padre?"

"Other ideas, no. But wait!"

"Ya got something?"

"Resurrection," the Priest said and smiled big.

"Don't he have to die afore that?"

"Yes, unfortunate. By the way, is Immanuel a Christian?"

Uzziah had been wondering the same thing himself. He didn't know. They had never talked much about God or Heaven or anything like that. He, Uzziah, was baptized, both christened and emersed. Christened when a child, then when he was twelve, he saw people down by the river. He'd been fishing and he thought maybe they'd had better luck than him. He went down there, and a man in a suit was standing in the river with the water up over his waist. What the hell? There was a line of people walking in, and he was—well, it looked like he was trying to drown them but wasn't being very successful. Each time he held somebody down, they'd come right back up again with a ridiculous smile on their faces, and some of them shouted hallelujah.

Those on the bank were singing a song. The words were, *when I went down to the river to pray, thinking about them good old days, and who would wear the star and crown, oh Lord, show me the way,* or something like that.

He liked the song, and he guessed it looked like he was in line 'cause when everybody else was dunked, the preacher motioned to him. He looked behind him like there was somebody else the preacher was motioning to, but it was him. He put down his cane pole and can of worms and waded right in. The man asked him some ridiculous questions. He could still remember them. *Did he renounce the works of Satan?* Well, heck, he never knew that he'd endorsed them. *Did he believe that Jesus was the Son of God?* What preacher would ask such a question? Then, he said, *"In the name of the Father, Son, and Holy Ghost, I baptize you."* Then he dunked him good.

"Immanuel?" the Padre said again.

"I don't know whether he's a Christian or not. I really don't."

"If you want to see yer friend on the other side, ya better find out, no?" the Priest asked.

"Yeah, probably," Uzziah said as he said goodbye to the priest and went to the plaza.

6

U zziah had barely walked into the plaza when a scream came from the doctor's office. He looked over that way, as did everyone else in the plaza. The bride of the Mexican captain came running down the stairs which led from the office. Her face was streaked with tears as she ran down the street. There was only one interpretation of that.

Still, Uzziah walked up the stairs and into the doctor's office just in time to see him pulling the sheet up over the captain's face.

The two men looked at each other—what was there to say.

"Ya want me to tell the colonel?"

"Sure, why not," the Doc said.

Uzziah went back down the steps as if he were about to go to his own funeral. He passed the captain's wife and a few of her relatives who were going to claim the body. There would be a funeral, and soon. The Church would be tied up with the Easter services, and

Uzziah imagined that the captain's funeral would happen tomorrow.

He rode Shadow on down to the Mexican military compound. When he dismounted, the gallows, the permanent gallows built of mortar and brick, sat at the back of the compound and seemed to be mocking Uzziah and Immanuel. He had to do something and something quick, or his friend would be having his own funeral after having his neck broken.

The corporal ushered Uzziah into the colonel's office without further ado.

"I'm surprised to see you back here so quickly," the colonel said with his Mexican accent.

"Yer man is dead," Uzziah said without seating himself.

"So, Captain Sanchez has finally sluffed off his mortal coil, has he?"

"Yep."

"Sit, sit." Uzziah sat and looked at the colonel. He wondered what the man had on his mind.

"I have the feeling that no matter what we do here, you will leave Taos with the feeling that your friend did not get a fair trial," he said as he was writing something on a notepad. "I want you to have this. Take it," he said, extending it across the desk.

Uzziah took the small sheet of paper and looked at it. There was a name and address on it.

It was the name Luis Pedro Manzello, the crooked lawyer.

"No, not him, anybody but him," Uzziah said very firmly.

The colonel looked at Uzziah as if he had just picked his pocket, and he probably had.

"Somebody else, anybody else?" Uzziah asked.

The colonel took the tablet, wrote something else, and passed it to Uzziah.

"Who's Augustus Fleming?"

"Believe it or not, he's a very good lawyer who happens to live in Santa Fe. It's not that far from here, just down through the valley which the Rio cuts and you're there."

Uzziah looked at the name again, then up at the colonel.

"Still, you don't think my friend will get off, do you?"

"No, he will hang, of that, I'm sure."

"So, why get this guy to defend him?"

"Well, he's the best in the area, and he's an Anglo. You'll leave with your friend's body and know that you did the best you could." The colonel seemed to be playing it straight now that he knew he wasn't going to make money.

Uzziah stood and put the lawyer's name in his vest pocket.

"Well, I guess I should say thanks. When do ya think the trial will be?"

"Tomorrow. Believe it or not, we have a courtroom right here at the military compound," the colonel said, smiling.

———

As Uzziah rode toward the deep-cut valley where the Rio cut its way south, he thought about how the Mexican military had everything they needed to dispense whatever justice they wanted to. They could arrest, they could try the accused, and then lead them out back and hang them. It was very convenient.

He had to ride night and day because the trial would be the next day. It was a good thing he had Shadow because he didn't think any other horse could have made the trip as quickly as he did. He was sitting in a café in Santa Fe the next morning, well, late morning and asking directions for the man on the piece of paper.

Turned out, the lawyer, Augustus Fleming, lived not far from the café. When he got to the address, he could see an older man, well, a bit older than Immanuel, sitting in his garden off the side of his adobe house. He was drinking coffee and eating rolls. He had a long white beard, and was built like he had been one strong hombre before he had gotten old.

Uzziah didn't bother to go to the door, he simply spoke up from the street.

"Augustus Fleming?" he sort of shouted.

The man turned his head toward the street, got up, and walked over to the iron fence that surrounded his garden.

"Yes?" he asked over the fence, looking directly at Uzziah.

———

He was directed back to the garden by a servant, an older Mexican woman who never said a word to him but handed him a cup of coffee before he went out on the patio.

"Good, Cilia got you a cup," the man said as he extended his hand.

"Uzziah O'Bannon," he said as they shook.

"You seem to already have the advantage on me, knowing my name and all."

"The colonel up at the military compound in Taos gave me yer name."

"That's probably not good. Does he want me to make another useless defense of an Anglo?"

"Yes, he does."

"Well, tell me about it?"

Uzziah explained that the trial was the next day, and if they were going to be there, then they needed to go now.

Augustus agreed, and with Uzziah's help, he hitched up two of the most beautiful white mules that Uzziah had ever seen to a curricle, a two-wheeled carriage built for speed.

"I ain't never seen a carriage like this here one," Uzziah said.

"Yeah, most people just have a single tree with these, but my two whites will make amazing time going up the river valley to Taos. You just wait and see."

Uzziah tied the stallion to the back of the curricle after Augustus made many compliments on the horse.

"Well, at least he'll be able to keep up with the whites," he said and clicked up the mules and they took off for Taos.

They rode the better part of the rest of the day, stopping for a snack that Cilia had made them. They watered Shadow and the whites there in the Rio Grande, then raced back up the valley.

"How come yer a doin' this and I ain't even showed ya any money?" Uzziah asked Augustus.

The older man looked at him, his beard flying over his left shoulder as he turned his head to Uzziah.

"Tell ya what, son, I never get tired of trying to beat these bastard Mexicans at their own game. The colonel knows this, and he never tires of mocking me. But someday, someday, we will beat the bastard," he said as he turned his head back to the mules and cracked the whip over them. His beard parted and half went over one shoulder and the other half over the other shoulder. He never touched the hides of the white mules with the whip, but they must have been touched at some point because the mere crack of the whip over them made them step-up.

The moon came up and showed itself into the valley of the Rio, and it made strange shadows across the road and the Rio looked like a ribbon of silver rippling in the moonlight.

"Don't the moonlight bother them?"

"No, no, they've made this trip so many times. I think they could do it with their eyes closed."

———

It was early the morning of the next day—they had traveled throughout the night—and honestly, Uzziah thought the old man would be tired and cranky, but the longer he went without sleep, the brighter he seemed.

They drove right to the café where Uzziah had eaten the majority of his breakfasts since coming to Taos, and obviously, he paid for the lawyer's meal. He was amazed at how much the old man ate. This only reinforced the notion that the man had been an ox when he was younger.

They drove to the military compound after breakfast and were sitting in the courtroom, waiting on the proceedings to begin.

"So," Uzziah asked, "ifn ya know you'll lose, why exactly did ya come up here?"

"It's two days before Easter, and if I can drag this trial out, then we'll get the Easter weekend. They won't try someone on that weekend, and maybe you can figure out how to break your friend outta this hellhole."

Uzziah thought about that for a moment, then realized that the last chance Immanuel had was him breaking him out, rescuing him, delivering him from the clutches of the Mexican government. He realized then that he had been thinking this way for the entire time. The lawyer had seemed a wasted effort, but now that the very lawyer he'd hired was telling him to break Immanuel out, well, he thought it was good to have everybody on the same page. He leaned in close to Augustus.

"Got any ideas?"

"You mean my plans for the trial?"

"Nah, how to break him out?"

Augustus laughed and turned to Uzziah. "My American friend, I will drag this out—that's honestly all I can do. The colonel already knows he's going to give a guilty verdict. The only thing I'm good for is a few more days for your friend to live. Breaking him out, well, that, my friend," he said as he pushed his finger into Uzziah's chest, "that, is your job."

The chamber door for the judge opened, and everyone present—which was Uzziah, Augustus, the captain's widow, and so many of the captain's relatives —stood as the judge entered.

Uzziah just about fell over. The judge was the colonel in a judge's robe.

"He's the judge?"

"Now yer getting the idea," Augustus said.

The prosecutor for the Mexicans was a smarmy-looking young Mexican lawyer with his hair slicked back, and his assistant was another of the same sort. In fact, Uzziah had to chuckle to himself, they looked like twins who might do tricks on bicycles or something.

From the other end of the courtroom, the door opened and Immanuel was led in. He was still in the same clothes he'd been arrested in, and Uzziah could smell him when the jailer walked him by the defense table.

Another door opened and six men walked in and sat down in the jury box.

"They done picked the jury?"

"Yeah, can you say kangaroo court?"

"Your Honor," Augustus said as he stood, "I object!"

The colonel/judge looked at Augustus and frowned. "And what is your objection?"

"We would like some white men on this jury of his peers if they are to actually be his peers."

"And why is that?"

"If any of you speak English on the jury, I have a ten-dollar gold piece right here for you," Augustus said, and the Jurors just sat there, looking straight ahead.

"When will you tire of that trick?" the judge asked.

"When you start getting a juror up here who actually wants my ten dollars."

"Objection overruled."

The trial went on in this manner. Every time Augustus thought there might be something to object to, he did. Each time, a bit more time was run out as the judge/colonel and Augustus argued over the finer points of a kangaroo court, complete with a kangaroo jury.

They didn't get far that day. They managed to charge Immanuel for the crime of murder, which Augustus vehemently objected to.

"I object, Your Honor. This man did not go into that cantina with the idea of murdering Captain Sanchez. He merely went in there to have a drink after completing the business he'd come to Taos to complete."

"Nevertheless, Captain Sanchez lies at the funeral parlor as we speak—dead!"

"Yes, after the defendant, Immanuel James Jones, was offended by the captain as he called his parentage into question."

"At which point, the prisoner turned and mortally wounded the captain!" The judge said.

"By simply hitting him in the face with a right hook. How many times, Your Honor, have you been hit in the face and not died."

"The defendant never hit me, and for that, I'm grateful. But he did hit the captain, and now the captain is dead."

The trial continued. The jury might as well have been asleep. Well, one of the six men was asleep, snoring.

"Your Honor, can you ask Juror Number Six not to snore so loudly," Augustus said, and that even got a chuckle from the family of the dead captain.

They made it through the rest of the day without getting very far. Witnesses had not been called, nor had the charges been substantiated by the prosecution. Augustus had dragged the heels of the court as much as was humanly possible. When they were taking Immanuel back to the jail, Uzziah spoke up.

"Your Honor, can I speak to the defendant?"

The colonel/judge was getting up to leave the courtroom, and he merely moved his hand by flicking the fingers on his right hand at Uzziah.

Immanuel stood there looking at Uzziah with an odd expression on his face.

"You okay, buddy?" Uzziah asked him.

"Introduce me," he asked.

"Oh, sure, Immanuel James Jones, this is Augustus Fleming."

"Pleased to meet ya, sir," Immanuel said as he shook hands with both hands since they were cuffed together. "Yer doin' a fine job," he added.

"Well," Augustus said, "under the circumstances, I guess."

"No, partner, ya got the man with the hatchet runnin' around chasing the chicken, and as long as the chicken's got a head and he keeps runnin', he's got a chance, right?"

"Right," Augustus said.

"Ya figured out to break me out, yet?" he kind of whispered to Uzziah.

Uzziah looked around the courtroom as if to chastise Immanuel for saying such a thing.

"Let's face it, pard, it's the only way I'll get outta this place alive."

"True," Uzziah said.

"I'm ready to go for plan *A*," Immanuel said right before the jailer took him away.

Augustus looked at Uzziah and cocked his head.

The jailer came over and took Immanuel away, and both men watched him leave.

"What's plan *A*," Augustus asked as they were walking out of the military compound.

"Well, it's a bit complicated. Where ya stayin'?"

"At the only place in town to stay, I imagine you're there, too."

"Nah, met a man, Randy, ya know him?"

"Can't say I do."

"Well, ifn ya don't wanna pay to stay, I imagine ya could stay there. Ya want me to ask him?"

"Nah, I like my comforts and my hooch. There's a bar at the so-called hotel. Come on, let's go have a drink, ya can tell me about plan *A*. What do you say?"

"Sounds good. I'll ride over."

———

Augustus had his curricle parked in front of the military compound. Uzziah untied Shadow, who was hip-shot and drowsy, and, mounting up, followed Augustus to the hotel. It was a small, ugly affair off the plaza. It only had one story, but directly in the front and across from the desk was a bar. Nice, wooden bar with a brass rail for your feet and a few stools scattered down the length of it. They sat and ordered two tequilas. It was the first tequila Uzziah had had since the afternoon of the fight. It tasted good.

"So, tell me about plan *A*," the lawyer asked.

Uzziah looked around the bar and besides the barkeep who was down at the other end, it was just the two of them.

Uzziah told him about the priest Martinez and how he had given this particular drug to the gypsy who feared for his life and how the doctor had declared him dead, and he got himself buried. But instead of Father Martinez digging the man up, he'd been called away into the mountain for a last rite, and by the time he got back, the guy had suffocated in his coffin.

"Boy, oh boy, trading in one medieval torture for a worse one, huh?" Augustus said, then he added, "So, ya told your partner about that, and he declined?"

"Yeah, maybe I told him too much," Uzziah admitted.

"Look, I like your partner, he seems like a square human being. Killing someone with one punch is more like something that would happen in the boxing ring. Was he ever a pugilist?"

"A what?"

"A boxer."

"No, well, not that I know."

"Doesn't matter. Like I said with the colonel/judge, it's always going to be a guilty verdict."

———

Uzziah rode back down to Randy's by the gorge. The wind was picking up and he would spend another night in the stables with Shadow.

Randy came walking out, he had a spoon in his hand and it had something on it.

"Howdy," Randy said. "Where ya been?"

"The captain's dead."

"I heard, so I imagine the *trial* began."

"Oh, yeah."

"I'm fixin' rabbit stew ifn ya want some," Randy said and offered the spoon to Uzziah, who licked the spoon.

"Tastes good, count me in."

They ate in the tiny kitchen which overlooked the gorge. Randy must have cooked enough stew for an army because Uzziah's plate was heaped full and so was Randy's.

"There's more ifn ya want it?" Randy offered.

"I'll be lucky to finish what ya gave me."

They sat and ate, the talk surrounding Immanuel and his chances which were slim to none.

"Have ya been thinkin' of the priest's medicine?"

Uzziah put down the fork and the spoon he used to eat.

"Yeah, I have."

"Good."

"Good?"

"Yeah, I was walking out by where the Penitentes were setting up their things for the sacrifice, and something occurred to me."

"Yeah, what was that?"

Randy motioned for him to come closer. He wanted to whisper in Uzziah's ear. Uzziah thought it a bit ridiculous, after all, they were a mile or so out of town, who could have heard him?

What Randy whispered was interesting, to say the least. It was a takeoff from the priest's original plan and it didn't involve putting Immanuel in a box and throwing hours of dirt on top of the box. Uzziah looked at Randy and grabbed the arm that was closest to him.

"My friend, you may be a genius, seriously," Uzziah said, smiling broadly.

There was a voice at the door of the old house, and both men jumped in their boots. Randy had been secretive, and it turned out there was good reason.

Uzziah and Randy walked out to the front door, and there stood Augustus Fleming, his curricle parked with the two white mules stamping their feet like they wanted to run some more.

"Am I too late for dinner?" Augustus asked and he was ushered in, introductions made, and they went back to the table. Randy piled another plate full and sauced it up, putting it in front of the lawyer.

"Ough, my favorite," he said and dug in.

"Randy was just sharing with me an alternative plan which involves the priest's medicine," Uzziah said placing an enormous bite in his mouth.

"Let me hear it," Augustus said as he continued to eat.

In a low murmur, Randy went through his alternative plan. Augustus listened carefully, and it was obvious he was thinking all the time.

"I believe this young man, here, has come up with the plan we need, but we'll have to have a decoy, and I think I can provide that. The Mexican Army must be kept busy so that no one sees what we're up to until it's done, agreed?"

7

There were just a couple of days before the weekend. It looked like Augustus might be able to stretch the trial out past Easter, but now the shoe was on the other foot. The trial must end, and the sentence of death must be given before Easter. That was paramount. But how could Augustus essentially throw the trial and not let the colonel know? His strategy would depend mostly upon the colonel/judge. Augustus knew that the Mexican colonel was a narcissist. He would rely on this love of the colonel for himself to propel the trial forward. Augustus must look like he hated what was happening, and maybe even that he had lost his edge in this game that he and the colonel played.

At court the next day, Augustus purposely came to court without sleeping. He was always drowsy and incompetent when he'd lost sleep, and he counted that, on this particular day, he would be just the drowsy, incompetent man he needed to be.

"Mr. Fleming! Mr. Fleming!" the colonel had to call

the lawyer's name twice before the man seemed to awaken.

"Yes, Your Honor?"

"Are you ready for the questioning of the witnesses?"

"Yeah, sure."

The witnesses turned out to be several men, two of them Mexican soldiers, who had been at that particular cantina the afternoon and evening when Captain Sanchez verbally expressed his doubt about the legitimacy of Immanuel's parentage.

They told the same story twice. Identical, like they had been rehearsed. Augustus listened, and when he cross-examined them, all he seemed to do was drive home the points the prosecution was trying to make.

The judge/colonel looked on with some suspicion, but when it became evident that Augustus's lack of sleep was causing him to bring a quick end to the trial, he simply sat up in his judge's chair with his chin resting on one hand and listening with a beatific look on his face.

Immanuel played his part when, after each questioning, he seemed upset and argued with Augustus at the defense table. The judge took all this in and relished it. The day had finally come when his defeat of the lawyer Augustus Fleming was certain, and things would not be drawn out.

Augustus even called his client to the stand, and all that accomplished was the fact that, indeed, Immanuel had hit Captain Sanchez as the two Mexican soldiers had testified to and that he was guilty as hell.

Both the prosecution and the defense gave their closing arguments, and Augustus kept calling

Immanuel Manuel, which was, of course, not his name. He had to be corrected twice, then the colonel/judge just let it slip. He smiled at his old friend, the lawyer, who seemed to have lost more steps than he had gained in the past year. As far as the colonel was concerned, he might never be bothered by this lawyer again, ever!

The six-member Mexican jury did not even leave the room. They simply put their heads together and then sat back down.

"Has the jury come to a verdict?" the judge/colonel asked.

"*Si, si,*" said the foreman of the jury.

"And that verdict would be?"

The jury foreman did not speak but simply drew his extended thumb across his throat.

"Tomorrow," the judge said, "you will be taken from your cell and brought here to the military compound, where you will be hung by the neck until dead." The timing was perfect, tomorrow would be a Friday, just the day they needed for the plan to succeed.

They took Immanuel back to the jail, and he was asked what he wanted for his last meal. He asked for a steak, a thick one, and potatoes, greens, and biscuits.

———

As the order was taken over to the café where Uzziah had taken almost all his meals, then the priest, Father Martinez, showed up at the jailhouse.

"What do you want?" the jailer asked.

"I heard about the verdict. I'm here to offer last rites to the condemned man."

Since the previous attempt to use the poison, which

makes a man seem dead, had happened years before, and the man did not live or appear anywhere else, no one suspected the priest. After Father Martinez was searched and the jailor found no weapon on him, he was shown back into the cell where Immanuel was. Right before the priest entered the cell, the jailer grabbed his money pouch.

"What's this?" the jailer asked as he pulled a vile from the coin purse.

"It's anointing oil for the last rite," Father Martinez said.

The jailer opened the vile and smelled it.

"Yuck!" he said as he pulled the vile away from his nose, "What's this supposed to do, make a man smell so bad, he wants to die?" he asked and laughed at his own joke.

The priest took back the vile, recorked it, and placed it back into his coin purse.

———

In the meantime, all the other players in this charade were in their places. Augustus had gone back to his hotel in dejected remorse. His plans were to leave Taos immediately and head home to Santa Fe. He had the stable hand hook up the matching white mules, and he waited until he heard the news. He sat in the bar and had a goodbye drink while he watched the doctor's office across the street.

The dinner was taken from the café to the jail, and Augustus realized it wouldn't be long now. He looked at his pocket chronometer and waited. About a half-hour later, the priest ran from the jail and headed up the steps at the doctor's. The doctor, his bag under his arm, came down the steps as rapidly as any man his age could and followed the priest to the jail.

There was a general commotion which evidently spread to the military outpost of the Mexican Army. It was time for Augustus Fleming to be seen leaving town. As he rode past the jail, he saw the colonel in his smoking jacket. He had been called from his house. It was an emergency. Augustus hurried on by, not wanting to see the colonel.

Meanwhile, the doctor was bent over the inert form of Immanuel James Jones, whose dinner had come from his mouth in a torrent of vomit and was splashed about the cell. Even Father Martinez had some of it on the bottom of his robe. Evidently, Uzziah had been notified because within ten minutes he showed himself at the jail. His performance as mourning his best friend in the world was rather convincing.

"What happened to him?!?" Uzziah asked, none too friendly-like.

"Senor, please, he was eating his meal, he choked, and then vomited his dinner," Father Martinez said, hoping that the amount of medicine he'd given him was enough to do the trick even if he did vomit.

"Will he be okay?" Uzziah asked the colonel.

"How should I know, as before, I am the colonel, not the doctor."

They both looked at the doctor, who was shaking his head and pulling the stethoscope off the chest of Immanuel.

The colonel took the instrument, placed the earpieces in his ears, and pressed the diaphragm with its bell against Immanuel's chest. There was a lot of commotion in the jail.

"Silencio! Silencio!" the colonel commanded, and it was like a tomb. He listened carefully, moving the bell of the stethoscope around on Immanuel's chest. Finally, he jerked the earpieces from his ears and handed the instrument back to the doctor.

"El esta muerto," the colonel announced.

———

Immanuel James Jones's body was taken to the root cellar beneath the café. The colonel was in the café in his smoking jacket, questioning the cooks and anyone else who had touched the food. The new plan was to take Immanuel up to the hill where the Penitentes had a man hanging on the cross and exchange his body for the body of Immanuel. Then, when the drug had worn off, Uzziah would pick him up, and they would escape back to their mountains. It was a plan that allowed them to use the medicine without putting Immanuel in a coffin and in the ground. It was the only reason he'd taken the medicine.

"We will bury your friend now!" the colonel announced as he walked into the root cellar. The curricle which they were going to carry Immanuel's body up to the Pentitentes' hill was just coming around the corner to the back of the café.

"Perfect timing," the colonel announced as the Mexican soldiers took Immanuel's body and put it in the curricle with Augustus.

Augustus looked at Uzziah, who shrugged.

The squad of Mexican troops accompanied the

curricle up to boot hill. There had already been a grave dug in anticipation of the hanging. It lay open, gaping in the moonlight as they drove up with Immanuel's inert body. The soldiers put the body in the wooden casket and, taking the ropes, they lowered the coffin into the hole, then rapidly began filling in the hole.

The thought occurred to Father Martinez that perhaps the last time, when he had used the poison to help his friend out, the colonel had known more than he had let on?

Regardless, the hole was filled in record time, with all the squad taking their turns at the shovels.

Uzziah's heart throbbed in time with each shovel-full that thudded on the top of the coffin. His friend was essentially buried alive! At least it was night, and he could come back after this and dig him up in time. At least, that's certainly what he hoped.

"You and you," the colonel pointed to two of his men, "You will stay here until the morning, *comprende*?"

The two soldiers nodded and, taking up their rifles, they tied their horses to nearby trees.

Now, what was Uzziah going to do?!? Within the next two hours, if the priest had been right and given him enough to swallow before he threw up, Immanuel would be awakening in his premature grave.

"Everyone else, everyone must leave now! If you are spotted near here, they shall shoot to kill, do you under-stand?" The colonel commanded. Obviously, he must know what the plan was, or he was one hell of a poker player!?!

———

They left and rode back to Randy's, where Uzziah paced the floor.

"What are we gonna do?" he shouted to Father Martinez, Randy, and Augustus.

"It was a good plan," Augustus said, "but we obviously didn't give the colonel enough credit. He must know what happened before. Did anyone see you dig up the body of your friend, the one who suffocated to death in his coffin?" he asked the priest.

"Maybe, it was daylight. I was more concerned with saving my friend than making sure no one watched."

"Great!" Uzziah said, "I never should have gone along with this. Shoulda just gunned my way into the jailhouse and taken our chances on the trail."

"You had no way of knowing," Augustus said, putting his hand on Uzziah's shoulder.

"So, you're just giving up, is that it?" Randy spoke from the corner of his place.

"Ya got any ideas?" Uzziah asked.

"Hell yes!" Randy said.

———

The two Mexican soldiers were young, but they were the best shots that the colonel had in his troops. They had been waiting alone on boot hill for the past hour. They were nervous, and that feeling was being communicated to their horses, who were restive. The moonlight was casting weird shadows and those two young Mexicans were crossing themselves every time they turned around.

Then, from the bottom of the hill, down where all

the original graves on boot hill were, there came a weird keening.

"*Qui paso?*" one of them asked the other.

They took up their rifles and pointed them down the hill.

Then, specters, three of them, rose from their graves, or so it seemed, and started walking toward them.

One of the men threw down his rifle and, grabbing his horse's reins, untied it from the tree and rode out of there.

The other gritted his teeth and took aim at the specters as they seemed to float up the hill toward him.

He fired and there was a plinking sound. He knew he'd hit the ghost, the specter, but it kept coming his way. He fired again and again at each of the three ghosts. Each time, he knew his aim was true, but the ghosts kept floating toward him. Their keening sounds growing louder and louder.

Finally, after emptying his rifle, he threw it down and mounted up on his horse, which was about to break away from the tree and escape without him. He rode off into the night, screaming.

The ghosts came up to the grave and threw off the sheets which had covered them. At least two of them did. The third collapsed beside the grave.

Uzziah and Augustus went to the third ghost and pulled back the sheet. They had all worn metal plates on their breasts, but Randy's neck had been hit by a ricochet and he was bleeding out.

"Randy, Randy," Uzziah said, holding the dying man's head in his lap.

"Do ya know Suwanee?" was all Randy sibilated.

There was no saving Randy. Uzziah sang the Stephan Foster song as he dug. By the time he'd finished the first verse, Randy's eyes were glazed over, barely reflecting the moonlight. Uzziah reached from where he was digging and closed Randy's eyes.

They dug, and within half an hour, they had Immanuel out of the coffin. He was still drugged, and for that, Uzziah was glad. The sunrise broke over the Sangre de Christos Mountains and shone on an empty coffin. It was Easter Morning.

They placed Randy's body in the coffin, lowered it back down, and covered the grave once more.

Augustus helped Uzziah put his partner's body over the saddle of Immanuel's horse.

"I think this is goodbye, my friend," Augustus said as he shook Uzziah's hand.

"*Via con Dios*," Uzziah said and kicked Shadow up.

Augustus ran back down the hill to his curricle and was driving toward Santa Fe when the first of the colonel's men, accompanied by the colonel himself, showed up at the gravesite. The soldier who had been brave enough to stay and shoot at the specters was with them. There was a heated discussion between him and the colonel.

"Dig him up! Dig him up!" the colonel commanded his troops.

Within half an hour, the grave was open, and the top of the coffin was taken off.

"Who is this?" the colonel asked.

None of his troops knew Randy. Why should they? He was obviously shot, and Uzziah and Augustus hadn't bothered to take the metal plate off his dying chest.

The colonel rode back to the Mexican outpost, got all his troops in the saddle, and rode north. He knew that's where those two mountain men would be headed. But he was dead wrong.

Uzziah, with Immanuel's body slung and tied over his saddle, had headed due west toward Apache territory.

The colonel had hired an Injun tracker to follow the two mountain men, and as they headed north toward the Sangre de Christos Mountains, the Injun rode back to the colonel.

"Travel north, then change, go west," the Injun said.

"West?"

"Si, Oeste!"

The colonel knew what lay west, and it wasn't the mountains that were safety to the two Americano hombres. No, what lay west was Apache territory. If they thought he could be discouraged by them traveling into danger, then they didn't know this Mexican colonel. He had known about the poison and had known what had happened the last time the priest had tried that trick. Once they captured the Americanos, he would take them back, hang them both, then hang the priest alongside them. He was tired of being afraid of a church that did not support his government.

8

It had been two years since Geronimo had been with Immanuel and Uzziah. He had grown into a strong youth and now commanded a cache of braves as they went out into the Arizona territory. It was simply his father's way of letting him know he was trusted as a chief. Geronimo relished the freedom of riding with his own braves, and he wanted to score a coup that would prove to his father, the real chief, that he was now a man.

As a youth, he had married and had twins with his beautiful wife. And yet, when he had raided into Mexico, Mexican troops had come to his village and killed his young wife and their babies. Their babies had been thrown into the air and caught on bayonets. When he returned from his raid, the Mexicans had left the babies as they had been caught. The rifles were stuck in the ground and the babies had slipped down to the barrels. Their mouths now dripped blood, not their mother's milk. It was said that for a few days, Geronimo had gone mad. He swore in Spanish and made a promise to the Great Spirit that he would annihilate as many Mexicans as he could before he died.

That afternoon, it was hot in the desert, and his men had stopped at a trickling stream to water their horses and themselves. A rider came in and his horse was galloping before he came to a halt beside their young leader.

They communicated in Apache and Geronimo became excited. It seemed two men were riding their way. Geronimo called for all his braves to mount up. They would chase down these white men and show them that this was Apache territory and they were not only not wanted but would soon know the pain of torture and death.

The braves, with their leader, rode to the top of a rise and looked down upon the desert where two riders were making their way west. They weren't traveling fast, but neither were they taking their time. They waited until the riders were past them so they could not turn around and go back to where they'd come from. When they were way past the rise the Apache were mounted on, they swooped down and gave chase.

———

Uzziah and Immanuel hoped that their ploy not to go directly into the Sangre de Christos Mountains would give them enough of a head start to outrun the colonel and his Mexican troops.

Uzziah had yet to tell Immanuel that he'd been buried alive. The original plan had been to hang Immanuel up with the Penitentes and pretend he was one of them on the crosses while the colonel and his men looked for him. Obviously, that hadn't worked out. And yet, and yet, Uzziah couldn't bring himself to tell his partner that he had, as a matter of fact, been buried alive and barely saved by Randy and his crazy ghost plan. He would tell him, he was sure, but not today, perhaps tomorrow, perhaps never!

"So, how long did I hang on the cross like Jesus?"

Uzziah looked at him and decided he would lie to his best friend in the world.

"Long enough to confuse the colonel and get you outta there."

"I wish I'd awakened on the cross, that woulda been somethin', wouldn't it?"

"Yeah, yeah, it woulda been, that's fer sure."

"What the hell!" Immanuel said as he looked behind him, "Had a feeling someone was back there."

They kicked up their horses who had been loping, and the gallop was a welcomed change of pace. They rode hard, and if Immanuel had had a horse as fast as Shadow, well, they probably could have outrun the Injuns. They had no idea that Geronimo was leading this war party, and as they got closer and closer to being caught, the leader of the braves began to suspect that the two men they were chasing just might be his old friends. He ordered his braves not to fire on the white men, but that did not keep them from screaming at the top of their lungs as they plunged toward their prey.

Uzziah and Immanuel rode hard into a set of hills and found a spot to make a last stand behind some boulders. It was cover, but the only water was what was in their canteens. They dismounted, putting their horses out of harm's way behind some boulders, and in an act that only mountain men would understand, gave their horses the last of their water. They poured the water into their hats, and the horses drank deeply. Uzziah took the spyglass from his saddlebags and, lying upon one of the bigger rocks, sighted in on the coming Injuns.

"They Apache!" he yelled.

Immanuel came up and lay down beside him.

"What's the chance Geronimo is with 'em, huh?"

"Hundred percent," Uzziah said as he handed the glass to Immanuel.

"Hot damn!" Immanuel screamed as he stood and waved toward the approaching Apache.

Several of the Apache braves couldn't resist, and they loosed arrows at Immanuel. He took one in the arm before he fell back down behind the rocks.

"What the hell are ya doin'!?!" Uzziah asked him. "There ain't no way they know who we is!"

Soon, they were surrounded by the screaming, shouting Apache.

Geronimo rode up to them and said something to one of his braves, who dismounted and quickly went to Immanuel's aid.

"My friends, I am having trouble believing that it is both of you," Geronimo said as he dismounted, embraced Uzziah, and looked at Immanuel. "You should never assume an Apache will not shoot," he said and laughed.

They wanted to talk more, but one of the Apache scouts screamed something to Geronimo, and when he joined him, he ordered everyone back on their horses.

As they rode off toward better cover, Geronimo rode up beside Uzziah.

"Who is chasing you?"

"Mexican soldiers," Uzziah said.

There was a gleam in Geronimo's eyes which Uzziah did not understand, like it was a good thing to be chased by fifty Mexicans armed to the teeth.

"We will count many coups, then!" Geronimo yelled back to Uzziah.

They rode toward a butte that was visible from where they were. The Mexican troops, led by the colonel, tried to catch them before they got to the butte, but it wasn't possible.

Geronimo led his braves and the two mountain men into a narrow chasm that entered an open space. Once inside, the Apache chief dismounted and was followed up the side of the canyon to a spot where they could look down upon the Mexican troops, who seemed to be disoriented.

"Finding the entrance to this box canyon is impossible unless you've been here before," the young Apache chief said, then he added, "We will toy with these men and make them sorry they were ever born."

Uzziah wasn't sure of the advantage they had being essentially caught in a box canyon with only one way in or out, but he had learned not to discount any Injun's wisdom.

That night, after they'd eaten a meager meal of jerked meat and biscuits that Uzziah had made in his Dutch oven, he and Geronimo went back up to the lookout point. Immanuel had been treated by one of the braves and was resting well.

Below them, the colonel and his men had made camp. He wasn't giving up simply because the mountain men and the Injuns had seemingly disappeared into thin air.

———

The colonel wasn't going to leave until he had those two Anglos in his possession. He would hang them himself, putting the nooses around their necks and pulling the lever himself. No one had ever tricked him like these two, and to keep the respect of his men, those two must die.

They ate well because one of his troops had killed several antelopes, and the men were in high spirits when they made their bedrolls. There were several guards posted around their encampment, and the colonel was sure that, in the morning, they would have better luck.

The Apache who snuck into their camp that night did so by crawling by the guards. Their mission was simple, bring havoc into the minds of the Mexican troops so that they would run, then they would be the pursued, and the Apache would be the pursuers.

In the early morning light, as coffee was being made by the Mexican troops, a scream, much like that of a woman, went up from the troops.

Geronimo and Uzziah were on the ridge again.

"Someone has found our work," Geronimo said, patting the sack which lay beside him and Uzziah.

"Work?" Uzziah asked.

The Apache chief simply patted the sack and smiled.

Uzziah opened the neck of the sack, and inside, there were the heads of two of the Mexican troops. He and Immanuel had been told the story of how Geronimo's young wife and his two little ones had been killed by the Mexicans.

Uzziah knew that the young Apache chief would have his vengeance, and he and Immanuel had been the bait to bring the Mexicans into the trap.

Inside the camp of the Mexicans, there was the closest thing to a mutiny that the colonel had ever experienced. Within half an hour of the headless soldiers being found, the men were talking of simply mounting up and leaving regardless of what the colonel wanted. The fact that this discussion was going on was mutiny enough.

The young trooper who was shouting to the rest of the Mexican troops that they did not owe their lives to simply chasing down two Anglos was standing on a big rock, giving his oration to the rest of the men. He took a big breath and was about to continue when a shot rang out. A hole appeared between his eyes and his body slumped and rolled off the rock.

The Mexican troop grabbed their rifles and were looking around at who had fired on them, then they saw their colonel standing tall with smoke roiling from his pistol.

"Anyone who wishes to leave may do so," he said, and the troops were confused until he finished his sentence, "simply by raising their hands and being shot on the spot."

Needless to say, no one raised their hands.

The troops spent the rest of the day riding around the butte, trying to find an entrance to the hole-in-the-wall hideout where the Apache and the two mountain men were hiding. By the end of the day, all they had accomplished was wearing out their horses. There was no water nearby, so the colonel had men take the horses to a stream that they had passed on the way to the mesa.

———

Geronimo was sitting up there with Uzziah and the two severed heads when three troopers left with the herd of horses.

"This is too great a prize not to take," Geronimo said.

They walked back down into the box canyon and the young chief gave orders to three of his braves, who immediately took off climbing out of the box canyon the back way.

"What have ya got in mind?" Immanuel asked Geronimo.

"You will see," the chief said, and that was the end of it.

———

The Apache are known for their ability to run nearly as fast as a dog trot. The three men Geronimo sent over the backside of the box canyon knew exactly how to get to the stream that the Mexicans would be searching for. They ran most of the day, getting there before the three Mexican troops found the stream.

The Apache waited until the horses had drunk well, then they attacked. The first of the Mexican troops took an arrow through his midriff and struggled mightily as he fell from his horse who was enjoying a drink.

The other two made for their backtrail, hoping to

get back to their compadres before they were taken, but as they rode away, two Apache stood up in front of their retreat. Arrows were let fly and they found their marks as the two remaining troopers made dust clouds as they fell from their saddles.

———

Geronimo, Immanuel, and Uzziah were sitting up on their lookout over the desert where the Mexican troops had camped.

———

The colonel was worried because it had taken the troops he sent with the horses way too long simply to water the horses and return. It was dusk now and hard to distinguish much in the desert light.

"Here they come," one of the Mexican troops said, and listening, yes, the colonel could hear the sound of the rataplan of hoof beats coming their way.

"Why are they running the horses?" he asked, a rhetorical question really since there was no one standing near him.

———

From their position at the top of the canyon, Geronimo and the two mountain men could see in the fading twilight the cloud of dust that was being raised by the stampeding horses. By the time the troopers figured out what was happening, it was too late. It has been said that a horse will not knowingly run down a man, but in the twilight, and the firing of the rifles behind them, they couldn't have cared less who or what was in front of them.

Geronimo had to give the Mexicans credit. They had tried to get out of harm's way, but the horses ran down the majority of the forty or so men who were left. Some of the men had turned in early and were trampled in their bedrolls.

Geronimo stood up and gave the wildest Injun cry that either Uzziah or Immanuel had ever heard.

"Now, we will go down and gather up the herd of horses and have fun with the Mexicans," Geronimo said, and the three of them went back down into the box canyon.

When the Apache made their way from the hole-in-the-wall entrance, there was hardly any resistance. Geronimo was happy that the colonel hadn't been seriously injured.

Several of the troopers shot at the Apache, but they were dispatched quickly and the rest surrendered. As they would find out later, it would have been best to go out shooting. Surrender is not something the Apache understand, or even care about.

9

The line of prisoners that were surrounded by the Apache looked like they were going to their deaths, and well, they were. The colonel was allowed to head up his column of men for the last time. Geronimo had a sense of humor that was pure evil. When they rode into the Apache camp, there was ululation from all the women, and the children were learning to gain coup by running up and hitting the prisoners on the legs with sticks. One child even stabbed a Mexican soldier in the leg, and was rewarded by cheers from all the villagers.

"It sounds like they're getting ready to have a big party," Uzziah said as they smoked with the big chief, Geronimo's father. His father was so proud of his son that, immediately, he gave him the big chief's headdress and he wore it for the rest of the celebrations. Geronimo was rewarded by many for his prowess and his ability to bring in prisoners. Gift after gift made their way to the new chief's feet. His chest was puffed up and many of the young women whispered promises of sexual

103

congress into his open ears. His smile was endless, it seemed.

"Let the party begin, old son," Immanuel said.

"They're gonna party with the captives?" Uzziah didn't quite understand.

"Yeah, you could say that. First, they will work themselves up into such a frenzy that no matter what atrocity they commit, it will seem minor. Some of the captives will be staked out for the sun to do its job, then others will be tied to posts, but before it's all done, there ain't gonna be one Mexican alive, that I can guarantee ya."

Uzziah watched as the Apache made special foods for the *party*, and everyone got their knives out and sharpened them.

"We have whiskey," Geronimo announced.

Uzziah looked at Immanuel.

"You may partake if you like," he said as he passed the bottle to Immanuel.

Immanuel took a hit, but Uzziah could tell that he had blocked the mouth of the bottle with his tongue, and no matter that he held the bottle high, very little got into his mouth. Uzziah decided he would do the same. He wasn't quite sure why they weren't drinking, but when the little chief went away with the bottle, he turned to Immanuel.

"Why ain't we getting' drunk?" he asked Immanuel.

"Because these savages are all notional, and you should always keep that in mind. What do ya think is gonna happen when they are through having their fun with the twenty or so prisoners?"

"The party will be over?"

"Think again, partner. There will still be two party favors left."

"You and me?"

"Now, yer gettin' it," Immanuel said, then he added, "So, whatever happens, keep yer wits about you because we may have to end up runnin' from the very ones who saved us."

"Ya think?"

"I know."

"Look, this will take a few days at the least. They will eventually kill all the prisoners, but they have as a people a belief that when men are tortured, they will show their prowess by gritting their teeth and taking it. They want these men to die good deaths, and they will do whatever it takes to give them the opportunity. Son, if the Apache were prisoners and being tortured, they would sing their death songs, spit at their torturers, and die with a smile on their faces."

"Really?"

"Old son, you watch and learn, and when the time comes, we will light out of here like two shucks on fire."

———

When the sun set, they began their festivities. The Apache knew that they were going to kill all the Mexicans, but what they didn't want to happen was for all of them to die quickly. They began by flaying one man who was staked down. They started with his privates and the man screamed bloody murder.

The children came to the man and were shown how to cut the skin just so and then peel it back so they could get a handle on the piece of skin and pull it the entire length of the arm, leg, or torso. The children laughed and played and took turns as the Mexican they were flaying begged them to stop. They laughed at his tears and spat on his face as they continued to do what their elders had taught them.

In another area, they had a man tied to a post, and then they threw knives at him. The idea was not to kill but to get as many knives in him as they could before he fainted. Uzziah counted fifteen knives that were stuck in his belly, arms, legs, groin, and neck until the man fainted. They took that prisoner down and revived him.

"He'll be burned alive later when almost all the others are dead. He'll think he's been saved and maybe even that he will be made a part of the tribe—and believe me, at this point, he would be willing to join them—but he screamed too much when the knives went in, they would never respect him enough to give him a weapon and let him fight with them," Immanuel explained.

All this time, the colonel wasn't harmed at all. In fact, he was stripped naked, and squaws led him around with leather thongs tied around his penis, balls, and neck. Whenever he tried to look away from those being tortured, the squaws would jerk on his penis thong, and he would cry out in pain, they would laugh like it was the most fun in the world. Those squaws led the colonel around to all the torture sights.

At one such sight, the corporal who worked for the colonel in his office was coaxed by a naked squaw who was very young into getting an erection. The naked girl slathered bear grease all over her beautifully naked body and lay on top of the young man as she writhed around on him, even sticking her breasts into his face.

He gladly licked her nipples, and fairly soon, he had an enormous erection, at which time she was thrown a knife with which she cut his erect penis from his body.

She picked up the severed member and stuffed it into the mouth of the soldier, who was obviously crying out in pain. He choked on his own penis, but before he choked to death, they pushed his penis down his throat and massaged his throat until he swallowed his own member. He tried to vomit, but they blocked his throat with a piece of hardened leather that they shoved into his throat. In essence, he was forced to swallow his own penis several times before he passed out.

"You men can watch this and still think of yourselves as men?!?" the colonel yelled at Uzziah and Immanuel.

The squaws laughed as they rather liked the reaction of the colonel, until he lunged at the two guests of honor, and they pulled his penis harness too hard and severed his member and testicles from his body. He screamed in pain, and the squaws laughed, picking up his manhood and passing it around to one another. One of the medicine men staunched the bleeding by placing a burning ember on the wound. The colonel passed out. They didn't want him to die just yet.

The horrors went on for two days. Several of the older soldiers died from their torture, and their bodies were thrown on a giant bonfire, where children and squaws danced around singing.

On the second day, Uzziah had gotten very little sleep, and he accepted the whiskey when offered to him. He just couldn't stand to watch in a normal state of mind. At one point, he was offered a knife to cut on the colonel, but he refused. The Apache didn't much like that, even though Immanuel had taken the knife away from Uzziah, pretended it was his turn, and cut both the colonel's ears off. He put them on a string of rawhide and wore them as if they were the prettiest necklace he'd ever had. At one point, he danced around the fire and came close to Uzziah.

"You'd better stop drinking and pick up yer game unless ya wanna be next," he whispered in Uzziah's ear.

———

By the time the third day arrived, most of the Apache had either passed out from the whiskey—Immanuel wasn't sure where they had gotten all the booze, but it was plentiful—or gone to sleep from exhaustion. Torturing people was hard work! Some of the torturers had passed out beside the very men they were torturing, almost curling up with their victims as if this had all been a great party. Immanuel was glad there weren't any Mexican women there, for he would have been hard-pressed to watch women being raped and their breasts cut off to make tobacco pouches.

Uzziah hadn't done what Immanuel had told him to do. He'd gotten drunk and passed out in the arms of one of the older women of the village, who looked like a small child when Immanuel took Uzziah away from her. He wasn't sure what Uzziah had done with, to, or for the old woman, but she had a smile on her face when Uzziah was dragged from her tent.

"What the hell, I liked her," Uzziah protested.

"Yeah, well, tomorrow morning ya'll be sober, but she'll still be old and ugly as sin," Immanuel said.

Through the fog of drink, Uzziah could see that

Immanuel had saddled up Shadow and his own horse and had a modicum of supplies that they might need till they got to the mountains.

"Hey," Uzziah slurred, "this gives new meaning to the phrase, the enemy of my enemy is my friend."

"Sort of," Immanuel said.

"Huh?"

"The enemy of my enemy is my friend, sort of," Immanuel said, and Uzziah laughed. Immanuel put his hand over Uzziah's mouth, "Old son, ifn we gonna make it outta here, ya gots to be quiet."

———

They tried riding fast, but Uzziah fell off Shadow twice. Each time, the stallion went back and looked down at Uzziah as if to ask, "You forget how to ride or something?"

Finally, when false dawn was cracking in the east, Uzziah seemed to sober up.

"Why'd we leave the party?" he asked.

"You've got to be kiddin' me."

"No, I wanna know why? That old woman could suck the silver off a dollar coin!"

"Well, we'll just call you silver cock from now on, how'd ya like that?"

"I accept the acclamation."

They had made the mountains, and Immanuel felt like he was finally back in his element. Here, at least, he had a couple tricks up his sleeve that even the Apache wouldn't suspect. They rode harder until noon, and then they were winding through pine grove after pine grove, down and up mountain streams, circling back and going over pure granite where it was almost impossible to track, except for the vomit which Uzziah seemed to have an endless supply of.

"Why'd ya let 'em bury me, partner?" Immanuel asked.

"Nobody buried you," Uzziah said and scoffed.

"Ya told me last night I did get buried, now yer tellin' me different?"

"Yeah, yeah."

"Yeah, yeah, yer tellin' me different, or yeah, yeah, ya buried me?"

Uzziah was almost sober. He looked at his partner now and he knew the man deserved the truth. It was just he wasn't willing to tell it.

"Was I or was I not buried alive?" Immanuel said, his voice raised to an alarming level.

"You had to be there."

"I was there, partner, I was the one in the pine box who got put six foot under."

"What do ya want me to say?"

"I want to know, after promising me that wasn't what was going to happen, it actually happened?"

"Extenuating circumstances," Uzziah said.

"Your use of yer 50-cent vocabulary does not impress me. Tell me why?"

"The colonel must have known what happened the first time the priest had done it and wasn't going to let it happen again."

"Paybacks are hell, ya know?"

"What paybacks? We dug ya up, we got shot at, and Randy was killed."

"Yeah, sure, all that talk about steel plates on yer

chest and the ghosties out to get the Mexican soldiers. I don't know, Uzziah, it all seems a bit far-fetched."

"Far-fetched or not, it's how it happened. You owe yer life to Randy. He was the one who came up with the *steel-plated ghosties* idea."

"Well, when I run into the son of a bitch in the next life, I will certainly shake his hand."

"You'd better," Uzziah said and could think of nothing else to say, then all hell broke loose.

Apache war cries and arrows flung all over the place. Uzziah and Immanuel kicked up their mounts and headed into an area with a lot of downfall. Mountain horses can navigate in just about anything. The last thing a man wanted to do was take his horse running through a bunch of downed trees, but that's exactly what they did.

Behind them they could hear the Apache screaming, but also, they could hear the snapping of horses' legs as they were unable to jump successfully between the downed trees. Uzziah winced each time he heard another horse go down, but Immanuel was taking the time to turn in the saddle and blow a couple of Apache off their horses before their horses broke their legs.

"Did ya see Geronimo with them?" Immanuel asked.

"Did I have time to look for him?" Uzziah answered as the group of Apache behind them thinned out, and they came upon a meadow that lasted till the end of a valley.

They took off and were making good time when, out of the side of one of the ridges, a group of horses came running at them.

Uzziah raised his Hawken, but Immanuel stopped him.

"They're us!" he shouted, and sure enough, when Uzziah took another look, he realized he was about to shoot into a bunch of mountain men. The leader, or the first guy to get to them, shouted at Immanuel.

"We seen ya was being chased by Apache. What the hell they doin' up this way?"

"You tell me, they had a lot of whiskey down at their camp."

"Mother of God, that's who robbed the hooch train," he said and he peeled off and directed the other fifteen or so mountain men back toward what remained of the war party.

Uzziah and Immanuel pulled up on a rise and watched.

The booming of Hawkens echoed off each set of mountains on either side of the meadow. Apache were dropping like flies until they turned tail and ran. It looked like the mountain men might follow them back to where they came from, but they stopped to take scalps and that was the end of the chase.

10

Back at their cabins, the men who had rescued them from the Apache war party and the two mountain men whose home it was celebrated. Evidently, old Geronimo had learned a lot from Uzziah and Immanuel when he'd stayed with them for that summer. Like where the booze was stored, when it came in, and where. He'd used that knowledge to take the whiskey train down and torture and kill all the teamsters who had braved it to come with the booze.

They partied, and everybody got drunk. Well, Immanuel had a bad habit of hiding booze away in different scathes, and he'd gone and brought back what they needed. Neither Uzziah nor Immanuel looked over the scalps that their friends had taken, and it was agreed between them that Geronimo's scalp was not among them. Not that it would have mattered to them, but then again, the enemy of my enemy and all that.

———

Uzziah had a drunken dream that night that he had married the old squaw who could suck like a boot caught in quicksand. He was relatively happy in the dream, and even though she was old, she managed to whelp him out some good-looking little Injuns who loved their pa.

When he awakened from the dream, the rest of the camp was either passed out or still sleeping. He saddled up Shadow and took a ride back to the valley where he and Leah had buried her father.

He knew where the grave was, and it didn't take him long to find it. He picked flowers and put them on the stones that he and the man's daughter had managed to roll onto his grave. It had worked, the critters hadn't bothered anything. The man was probably intact, except for the bullet holes that eventually killed him.

He decided he would stay there that night. He'd had, in the last couple of months, enough of the human race. He made himself a dinner of jackrabbit, which had only been curious about who Uzziah was and found out what he looked like from the inside of his stomach.

Uzziah was no fool, and he realized that things kill other things to stay alive. That was the nature of things. But those three days with the Apache had soured him to how cruel human beings could be to each other. He knew that it was their culture that had taught them to be that way. Heck, even the little bastards were getting into the torture and enjoying it.

Then, the way the sun set itself, he thought back to the little Methodist Church in the Shenandoah Valley where he grew up. He'd seen a similar sunset one afternoon outside the church, well, in the woods at the back of the church.

He liked the minister's daughter, her name was Eloise, and she liked him. He'd taken some shine his pa had made and he and Eloise had drunk every bit of it. She got so drunk that she stripped off her clothes and went bathing in the creek. He'd joined her, and they played in the water, then ended up kissing like he'd never kissed anybody.

On the sandy shore of that little stream, she'd laid down and he was about to mount her when she said the strangest thing.

"Your chest, it reminds me of my pa's."

That's all she'd said, but it put a new light on what they were about to do. Made him wonder about the Methodist Minister, and then, he had lost what he was about to put inside her.

She didn't care, but cuddled up there in the sand and they'd fallen asleep naked, listening to the babbling of the brook.

Funny, the things that can come back into a person's head at the strangest time. If he had made love to that little bit of a girl, he probably would have married her, and they would have had a passel of kids, and who knows what would have happened then?

Instead, he was a virgin till he met the one whose name he could no longer say. He did whisper that name just loud enough for him to hear it over the crackling of the flames in his cookfire. She was the kindest soul he'd ever met, and it didn't matter to him what went into her when he wasn't with her. She loved him, too. He wondered what would have happened if that undersheriff hadn't gutted her the way he did?

He lay beside the fire until it had reduced itself to

embers, and when a chill came on him, he rolled into his blanket and watched the coals till he slept.

In the morning, he caught several trout in the stream in the meadow, said his goodbyes to Leah's pa, and rode back toward the cabins. He had to laugh to himself about that winter with Leah, both he and Immanuel trying to be so proper with her that neither of them even got a taste.

Maybe that was the difference between the Injuns and the white man. The former were all instinct and nerve, the latter had their instinct and nerve covered by the saving grace of Jesus. It wasn't that that covering was bad, it just made them different in every shape and form. And he knew awful things had been done in the name of religion, but it didn't change the way his heart felt about the Holy Spirit residing there. His thoughts drifted back to the *party* that the Apache had had, and he almost lost his breakfast. He choked it back down and said a little prayer about being glad he was who he was, regardless of who anybody else was.

EPILOGUE

When he got back to the cabins, Immanuel wasn't there. He'd left a note saying he would be back in a month or so, and if Uzziah didn't mind would he set the traps out if he wasn't back by the fall. Not another word. He wondered where he might have gone to and prayed it wasn't the burying of his partner which had set these wheels in motion. People do the strangest things for the strangest reasons.

What Immanuel's absence did do was make Uzziah self-sufficient. He didn't have to second guess himself, he just went about the business he knew needed to be done, and that was that.

Summer turned to fall, and still no Immanuel. Uzziah was sure that what had happened in Taos had somehow gotten to Immanuel more than either of them could have imagined. Yes, he had allowed them to bury the man while he was still alive, but what was he supposed to do? The colonel had been right there with his troops. He couldn't exactly grab Immanuel and ride off with him. Everyone thought that he was dead, that was what saved him from the noose.

He couldn't think about it, so he got busy. He started laying the traps out and curing the pelts that he harvested. It was a bloody business, but it kept his mind off his, yes, best friend.

The weather was colder this fall than it had been the one before. Who knew, maybe this was the way it always was in the fall, and Uzziah had simply been there during a couple of warm autumns?

He turned the cabin with the pot-bellied stove into a drying room for the pelts. He kept a low fire in the stove and made an array of lines that crisscrossed the ceiling. It was working well, and the pelts may not have been plush, but what they lacked in luster, they made up for in quantity.

He didn't spend all his time working. There were opportunities to rest and study his Bible, something that he'd done his entire life. A lot of people think that having a large family with so many brothers and sisters meant that you had no time for yourself. And yet, it was the very fact that he was surrounded by so many that he sought out opportunities to be alone. His spirit demanded it. Perhaps that was what had driven him west. The older he got and the more responsibilities that were expected of him, the less time he had for— what would his pa call it—daydreaming, that was it.

The same creek he'd taken the minister's daughter down to, well, perhaps in retrospect, she had taken him down there, but it wasn't the first time he had been to that secluded spot. He'd gone down there many, many times after his chores, and he always took the Bible he'd been given.

One afternoon, after he'd been in Genesis and reading about the flood, he'd fallen asleep beside the brook. It must have been the sound of the water because he dreamed he was one of the lost.

Noah was standing on the deck of the ark and watching all the people who were doomed. He was calling out to Noah, and the man actually looked directly at him. He could feel the pain in Noah's heart. He was a good man, and he hated with all his being seeing those who had been his neighbors destroyed. A lesser man would have gone into the ark, had his wife fix him a sandwich, and forgotten about those who were not included.

He was sitting with the Bible on his lap and thinking when he heard someone approaching. He was hopeful that it was Immanuel, but it turned out to be a curious raccoon. Then, he remembered the pigeons, and he wondered if there had been a message from Oscar and Ophelia. He went to the coop, and only one of the pigeons was there. They had left the door to the coop open so that they could come and go as they pleased.

Both the pigeons had the small metal container on their legs, and gently he got the pigeon out, and the container had no message. Then, the second pigeon arrived and settled in, cooing to its partner. He corralled the second tumbler pigeon and there was a tiny piece of paper in the small packet which was attached to its leg. He unfurled the small note and it was an invitation to a wedding. It seemed that Leah was getting married to Willet.

Uzziah had no way of knowing exactly when this particular pigeon had arrived, or if it had been in and out of the coop a dozen times before he found the message, or exactly when the wedding was to be. Still, the fall season for gathering the pelts was almost over. He had plenty of pelts and decided he would close things up and take the trip to see if the wedding was still on.

He closed up the cabins as best he could—well, to tell the truth, he shut the doors. If someone came along and took the pelts, they were no good sons of bitches and that's all there was to it. He did so want Immanuel to see the work he'd done, but be that as it may, he left riding Shadow down the mountain and heading for Oscar's place.

———

The first night out, there were lights overhead, and they were gyrating and green. He could hear something coming off of them, and as he listened, he realized these were the northern lights he'd read about once in a book. But they weren't in a book now, they were real and overhead. The sounds they made were like the static that comes off a dry sweater when you jerk it off. He tried to sleep but couldn't keep his eyes closed long enough to do so. Those lights, they must be some kind of portent, at least, he was sure that's what some people thought. Maybe they were a celebration of the marriage feast they'd been invited to, maybe not?

Finally, after trying to sleep for what seemed hours, he decided his time would be better spent by riding under those lights on the way to Oscar's settlement. He wondered if they had finished Willet's cabin and what other work they'd done.

The morning of the third day, he recognized the forest around Oscar's and knew he was close. He could hear music, fiddle music, some guitar, and maybe even a harmonica. He wasn't sure about the last instrument though.

When he made the turn in the road, he could see that the settlement was in full celebration. Evidently, the wedding had just happened or was about to happen. He rode in, almost undetected, but Ophelia saw him as he was putting Shadow away in a much bigger barn than he remembered. That woman, she was so strong. How she'd gotten over being raped like that was beyond him. Women were certainly amazing creatures. The music stopped, and even inside the barn, he could hear a voice that sounded like it might be the preacher, he wasn't sure.

"All right, everyone gather around and let's tell God what these people intend to do," the voice said.

As he was about to walk from the barn, he noticed a big mare eating oats. By God, if it wasn't Samson. How in the world? Out of the barn and shaking his head about the big mare that didn't need to be led, he was greeted by Ophelia, who handed him a glass of punch.

"Thank ye," he said, and she hugged him.

He downed it. He was fairly thirsty.

"My, my, what delicious thing is in this punch?"

She smiled up at him.

"It's a celebration drink," she said and wound her arm around his waist and walked with him over to where Oscar was standing, smiling at his brother who was standing up by the preacher.

The music started again, and this time, it was "Here Comes the Bride."

Uzziah looked where everyone else was looking, and there Leah was, on the arm of a good-looking older man who was wearing a new set of deerskins. Uzziah couldn't believe it, the older man was Immanuel. He had his hair in braids on the sides and beads and feathers were braided in with the hair. Uzziah had never seen his partner, if he could call him that, look quite so handsome.

The music continued as they walked down the separated crowd of people. It must have been everybody within a 100-mile radius. Leah was stunning in a lace dress, which Uzziah bet that Ophelia had made her, but he left room to be wrong about that. Leah had made curtains up at the cabins, that was what had started her journey back down to the hill country.

He wished Immanuel would look his way, he sure did miss the man, and he wanted to hug him something terrible. They walked right up to the preacher, who had a flat, black hat that some call a buckaroo Stetson.

"Who gives this woman in holy matrimony?" the preacher asked.

"I do," Immanuel said, and Uzziah could hear emotion in his partner's voice. Well, good for him. Maybe almost being buried alive had opened up some channels in the man's heart.

Immanuel handed over Leah to Willet and walked away. Willet was dressed well for a mountain person, pressed shirt, new pants, polished boots, and a good-looking deerskin vest. Uzziah thought he recognized Immanuel's handiwork in the vest. He secretly wondered how long the man had been here?

The preacher read the 13th Chapter of Saint Paul's first letter to the Corinthians, and everyone listened respectfully. He then went on to say that they were gathered in God's presence to see these two good people joined together in the sight of God and all these witnesses. He heard the man say what God had joined together, let no man put asunder.

"That's you and me," he heard a whisper in his ear. Turning, he saw Immanuel standing beside him.

"What's you and me?" Uzziah asked.

"Two people that God has put together," Immanuel said and smiled.

They put their arms around each other's waists, and really, Uzziah didn't hear much of the rest of the ceremony. His eyes filled with tears as he realized that Immanuel had gone past his anger at being buried alive, and when he turned and looked at the man, he, too, was silently weeping.

AMBUSHED

1

The party had lasted for three days. It wasn't intended to last that long, it simply did. Some of those invited had brought their own moonshine. That probably had something to do with it. Uzziah and Immanuel had seen each other from time to time. There was a makeshift dancefloor of lumber and they had waved to each other across it as they danced, sometimes with someone, then as one day became night and the next day the same, they just danced. For big men, they had light feet.

The morning they left, they did so not because the party was exactly over, more because they just couldn't drink anymore. There was a lot of snoring going on. The women had stayed more or less sober, because the kids had to be taken care of, and someone had to do the cooking. Uzziah and Immanuel said their goodbyes to Ophelia Blanchard and promised to keep the messages coming from the tumbler pigeons. They told her to give Oscar their best. Two-Jays, a.k.a. Charlie, was hanging onto Immanuel's leg, and Ophelia had to pry him away.

He didn't cry, but stuck out his arms to the big mountain man.

"What can I say, kids like me," Immanuel said as he mounted up.

They traveled for a day and a half before it happened. They should have been more alert, they should have seen them coming, but they didn't. Later, Uzziah would blame it on his foggy mind, that moonshine had been awesome, but it wore off slow as hell.

The first shot hit Uzziah and threw him out of his saddle. Shadow went just a little further before coming back to him. He was hit in the shoulder and was bleeding badly.

Immanuel was off his horse and headed for some cover when a hatchet hit him in the back of the head. Lucky for him, it was the flat side and thrown from quite a distance.

When he woke up, he wasn't sure how much time had passed, maybe a couple hours, maybe longer. He found Uzziah down by the stream, washing out his wound.

"What happened to yer clothes?" he asked Uzziah.

Uzziah looked up, his eyes rimmed with pain, and chuckled. "The same thing that happened to yers."

"My party clothes!" Immanuel yelled as he realized he was dressed only in his trapdoor union suit, the same as Uzziah. "I wondered why the rocks felt so hard," he said and looked down. He was without his boots.

"Those varmints took everything," Uzziah said.

The two men had their trapdoors on and nothing more, no hats, no guns, no nothing, not even their boots.

"Well, old son, not quite," Immanuel said, pulling up the right leg of his long johns. There, strapped to his leg, was a Bowie knife.

"I never seen that afore!"

"Have you ever seen me naked?"

"Thank the Lord, no."

"Well, that's why."

"They wasn't mountain men, or they would have taken my Bowie," Immanuel said.

"Well, they was probably so busy loading everything else up they just forgot. Besides, if ya had up and died on me and I was to bury you, I wouldn't knowed about that knife," chimed in Uzziah.

Immanuel just looked at Uzziah.

"Whatcha lookin' at me thataway fer?"

"How easy they ferget," Immanuel said.

"Fergit what?"

"Ya done buried me down Mexico way, 'member?"

"Oh, that, that was..."

"Yeah, yeah, we both knows what that was!"

"Are ya never gonna let that go?"

Immanuel just looked at Uzziah and didn't say a thing.

Uzziah was still bleeding. He'd cleaned the wound, it was a through-and-through—lucky there—but he couldn't staunch the blood.

Immanuel disappeared for a bit and returned with some plants. Uzziah knew some of the plants, Immanuel had meant to teach him more, but life gets away from you sometimes.

There was a set of boots lying near where Immanuel had awakened.

"Hot damn! They didn't take my boots!" Immanuel yelled out.

"Maybe they thought they was buckets?" Uzziah joked, laughed, and grimaced at the same time, grabbing his shoulder.

"Take her easy, partner."

"Well, where are my boots?"

"Look, ya wear an average size, well, old son, that's a size just about any man can wear, but me," he continued as he slipped on his gun belts, "with a boot this size, a normal man'd be swimmin' in them all day long,"

He stood up and stomped his socks in place in his boots.

"Now I feel like a man," he said. "Hey, and lookie cheer, there's the shammy," he said as he bent down and picked it up. "Flint ain't there, but I betcha..." he said as he looked around. "There she is!" He bent down and picked up the flint that he'd rolled in the shammy. "We can start a fire now."

He made a fire, found a scooped-out piece of tree bark, and boiled some water. He cleaned the wound—both sides—and, boiling some of the herbs and plants he found, made a poultice. He wrapped it around Uzziah's shoulder the best he could with some willow vines.

"Is that comfortable?"

"Hell no, feels like ya done cut the circulation off in my arm."

"It'll have to do 'til we find something else."

The two men walked the rest of the day, stopping often because of the blood loss that Uzziah had suffered, plus Uzziah was having trouble not stepping on something painful. Immanuel felt bad for his partner, tough enough getting shot, but hiking without boots, well, Immanuel figured those hombres who did this to them were about the lowest form of animal there was. They'd better hope he didn't catch up with them.

———

They tracked the men who had done this to them, naturally. From the hoof prints, there must have been at least six of them, and they rode shodden horses, so they weren't Injuns.

The morning of the second day, they came upon a cabin set way back in a holler. There was smoke, too much smoke, coming from the rock chimney, and when they spied the place from afar, there were their horses and six others. Some of the men were eating breakfast by a fire built outside the cabin, they counted three. The others were somewhere, maybe in the cabin?

There was nothing they could do until nightfall. They planned to sneak in like the half-Injuns they were and take those bad hombres down, but disappointment followed that idea like a faithful dog. Not an hour later, while it was plenty light, they shucked out of there, screaming and hollering.

Uzziah guessed that one of the bad bunch had probably tried to ride Shadow, but the result wasn't good. Yet, they knew he would get a good damn price somewhere. Both he and Immanuel's horses were still saddled, just as they had been at the attack.

They waited for about an hour before they approached the cabin. You never knew when somebody would come back. They approached the place like the bad hombres were still in there, and when they finally pushed open the door, the place was a wreck. The old man who had lived there, God knew how long, was dead as a possum, but there were some clothes around. Both men proceeded to get dressed after a fashion. Unfortunately, the old guy who was killed was small. Both mountain men looked as if they were wearing or trying to wear children's clothes.

The pants came about three inches above Immanuel's boots, and ropes had to be used to secure them around the waists, which were considerably bigger than the little old man. They simply cut the sleeves off the shirts so they could move their arms and eventually had to slit the arm holes so they could move more freely.

"Well, don't we look ridiculous!" Immanuel commented.

"Let's bury the poor old guy. Why would anybody just kill to kill?" Uzziah said, still looking ridiculous in the old man's clothes but choosing to ignore his partner's comment.

Then, in the corner behind the door, Uzziah spotted something.

"Hey, hey, hey," he said as he hobbled over and picked up the pair of boots. "They look like they might fit," he said as he limped over, picked up a turned-over chair, and sat down.

They were a bit snug. It seemed the old man might have been short and thin, but he had himself a pair of feet.

Night was falling, and they took the old man's body out behind the cabin. Immanuel found a shovel, and, since he was the only one able to dig, he dug a grave, not too deep, but with rocks on it, it would keep out the coyotes.

"Father, this cheer old man didn't do nothing to nobody, but they messed him up anyway. Who does something like that? We'd like to commend this man's body to the hole I done dug, and hope that when Jesus opens the book of life, he'll find the old man's name, and beside his name will be all the good things that he's done. Amen."

Immanuel rolled him into the not-so-deep grave and then filled the hole and piled rocks on top. It didn't look too bad. Uzziah looked terrible. He was sitting by a tree and had gone to sleep, but his color was terrible. Immanuel took him back to the cabin and built a fire. He was sure those arsewipes weren't coming back now.

He cleaned up the old man's bed as best he could, and as the temperature dropped outside, they stayed warm and cozy. Immanuel made Uzziah some more medicine for the gunshot wound, and when he took the old bandage off, the wound smelled bloody but fine.

"Ya just go to sleep, partner, yer wound looks okay, ya ain't lost that much more blood. Tommary, I'll kill us a rabbit and we can get some real food in our bellies." He looked over and Uzziah was asleep. "Well, maybe tonight?" he said, and taking the old man's coat, which almost fit—nobody likes a big coat that's too tight—he wandered out into the night.

———

When Uzziah was waking up, he had a dream that his ma had found him in the woods all busted up and roasted him a rabbit. That dream was so real that when he opened his eyes, he still smelled the rabbit roasting.

"How ya feelin'?" Immanuel was sitting next to the stove, and he had rabbit meat on sticks, and they were propped up and roasting nicely.

"Where'd ya find the meat?"

"They heard ya was sick, so they came by and committed suey-cide fer ya," Immanuel said without breaking into a smile.

The rabbit was good, and both men regained a bit of the strength that they usually had.

As they were finishing up, there was some movement outside the cabin. It was still early, and they didn't know what to think. Immanuel signaled to Uzziah that he was going outside with the Bowie knife to see what was what. He stood by the door, ready to snatch it open, just in case there was another one of them who hadn't made any noise.

"Hee-haw! Hee-haw!" the braying came, and when Immanuel opened the door, there stood a fourteen hands high jackass, or donkey, he wasn't sure which. He went out there and the fella was friendly enough. He had the two stripes on his back which crossed at the shoulder going down each leg.

"This cheer's a Jesus donkey," Immanuel exclaimed.

He looked in and Uzziah had a rabbit leg in his hand and was gnawing away at it.

"Whatcha mean, Jesus's donkey?"

"There's cheer two stripes on his back crossing each other at the shoulders, making a cross. Legend has it this was the kind of donkey Jesus rode into Jerusalem, right before they crucified him."

"That don't sound like a good omen."

"Are ya kiddin' me? You can ride this beast and I'll walk. We'll make twice as much time today."

———

And that's what they did. Immanuel found a lead rope and halter in an almost demolished barn. The bad hombres hadn't done that, time had. They were quite a sight, the two of them. Their clothes were too small, which accented their boots, and Immanuel had threaded the rope around his waist to carry the knife scabbard. He had the lead rope in one hand and was pulling the donkey along. The Jesus donkey wasn't really glad about taking a walk.

Immanuel found the trail of the six hombres fairly quickly, and as long as it didn't rain, they could follow them to hell, if necessary.

2

The six men who had done all this—and much, much more—were riding west toward the Rockies. If someone was on their trail, they didn't quite care. These malcontents had gotten together in a saloon where Francis Grossman was about to get in a fight. Francis was the middle son of a rabbi in Galveston, Texas. He had never been a good boy. His father, Rabbi Grossman, was a strict and uncompromising man. He had five children—two boys and three girls. The boys had been good workers, but Francis, and he did not like being called Frank, started going downtown where he saw sailors from all over the world, where the women were there for one reason and one reason only, to give pleasure to men.

But that was years ago, when Francis was younger, much younger. This particular fight had something to do with a man saying something about Francis's nose. He did have a hawker, but most men stayed away from obvious faults of another man, most men mind their own business. But the man down the long bar from Francis had spoken right up.

"Betcha can fly with that nose of your'n," the man had said.

Well, Francis didn't pay attention at first because it wasn't a very good insult. How can somebody fly with their nose? But Francis knew what the man was getting at—he had a nose like a hawk. Francis let it go for a bit, but the next insult hit home.

"Yer a no-good yella-bellied foreigner, ain't ya?"

Yes, his family had emigrated long ago, and yes, you could say he was from foreign extraction, and Francis liked to make that distinction, but to say that Francis was yellow? Nah, just not so.

Five other men, who were like Francis, saddle-bums mostly, but they liked what all men like—whiskey, whores, and gambling. They had been watching this man at the end of the bar trying to goad this big man with a really big nose, and they weren't liking it one bit.

Ostensibly, they were playing cards, but these five had been traveling together for some time, and they were only small time, what they needed was a leader. Not one of them had any idea about having fun that was against the law and possibly actually getting away with it. So, when the well-known citizen at the end of the bar started ragging on Francis, well, their evil hearts went out to him. At one time or another, they had all been bullied, and that's why they were together—strength in numbers. Before it had all begun, they had taken the wang leather off their hammers and were simply waiting.

Francis was about to leave. Yes, he was going to take water, because every insult this guy threw at him was laughed about by just about everybody there. In other words, the man was well-known and liked, because he really wasn't that funny.

"Ya know," the obnoxious man at the end of the bar began again, "at first I thought ya was a no-good Mexican, but I heard ya speak. Ifn ya was a greaser, then yer English wouldn't be so good. That's why I think yer not only a foreigner, but an honest-to-God rope sucker!"

Well, everybody liked that one, all men are afraid that they just might like what other men could do to them, but they aren't strong enough to admit it. Any time they get the chance to think that someone is in that way, well, that throws all the guilt off them onto somebody else. In biblical times, it was known as scapegoating.

Francis didn't say anything, but he turned, and when he turned, he, too, took the wang leather off his hammer, and everyone else at the bar backed away, except one man, and when that man turned, he had a five-pointed star pinned to his chest.

"My friend," the sheriff said, "whatever has happened here this afternoon ain't worth yer life. Ya understand that, don't ya?"

"I will not take water from the drunk at the end of the bar," Francis said in a voice like he was teaching everybody English.

"Fer a foreigner, he speaks fairly good, don't he, Ned?" the drunk at the end of the bar said to the sheriff.

"Yeah, here's more information for ya foreigner, that there drunk at the end of the bar is my brother-in-law. Ya know he's married to my baby sister."

"Well, that is touching. I hope she said goodbye and good riddance to him this morning because the next time she sees him, he's going to be in a pine box," Francis said, his hand slipping down by his Remington revolver.

"Ya don't get it, stranger. My brother-in-law is well-liked," the sheriff said.

It was then that Francis did something that none of those five hombres sitting at the poker table, not really playing poker, had ever seen. He insulted and drew at the same time. It was so wonderful to see someone just throw it in the face of the law and the town and those good upstanding citizens that, spontaneously, those five jumped up after the initial draw and blasted every man jack who was trying for Francis.

"Well, there's one person here who doesn't care for him," Francis said, and his Remington was out so fast that the sheriff stood there as the first shot from the Remington whizzed by the sheriff's midsection and drilled a hole in his brother-in-law's heart. The man fell like he had been a puppet and someone had cut the strings.

The sheriff started to draw, but he was gifted a beautiful headshot that blew his brains from where he was standing in the middle of the bar all the way down to where his brother-in-law had been standing. In fact, a gob of brain skidded down the slick mahogany bar, balanced at the end, before gravity got it, and it dropped to the floor beside the puppet with the cut strings.

Well, he was only one man, so everybody who was anybody grabbed for iron. But then there was the table of poker players who weren't playing poker, and they felt like it was a free day at the circus, and this was the greatest shooting booth they'd ever seen.

One after another, men drew and were put down by either Francis or one of the five poker boys.

When it was all said and done, that saloon looked like a slaughterhouse. There must have been close to twenty bodies, and not all of them were dead, but they were down and moaning. Anyone who hadn't been shot was gone. The place emptied out like the ark on Mount Ararat. They fled, that's what they did.

Francis looked at the five hombres who had stepped up and helped him, and he said two words, "Come on!" and all six went for their horses.

They didn't flee out of town because that's not the way Francis did things. He rode nice and easy as they were about to kick up their mounts and get the hell out of Dodge. Not Francis, he mounted up, lit a cigarette, then trotted out of town.

Well, this was braver than what he'd done at the saloon. To ride with impunity out of a town where you had just orphaned kids and widowed mothers. It was too good to be true. They now had a leader as they followed in behind him and trotted gracefully out of town without a single shot being fired at them.

Those six men now were riding toward the Rockies, as stated before. They feared no one because, so far, there hadn't been anybody who wanted to mess with them. Their first mistake as a gang of murdering thugs had been to cross Immanuel James Jones and Uzziah Ferguson O'Bannon.

If anyone had told them that their deaths were on foot behind them, that the mountain men they had robbed and left for dead had, at the very least, recovered and were walking to get them, well, they would have had a good laugh.

And yet, Francis Grossman had at that very moment a chill go down his spine. He felt sure that someone had walked over his grave. He looked around, and the gang of five, the Poker Brothers, he called them, were joking and cavorting with one another. Francis could see no one on their back trail. *Still, something not good this way comes*, Francis thought to himself.

———

Uzziah was getting worse. His color wasn't good, and Immanuel wished he had his saddlebags with all his plant medicines in them, but he didn't. So far, Uzziah had managed to stay atop the donkey, and the little critter wasn't objecting anymore, he was simply going along with the men, glad to have a human around. When they stopped for lunch, if you could call it that, Immanuel put Uzziah down where he was going to build a fire and tied the little guy up to a tree that was surrounded by sweet grass. He appreciated that as he went to munching the grass and did so the entire time they were there.

Immanuel's luncheon spot had been near a stream that looked like it might have some trout in it. He had once had an Injun wife who could stand in a stream for hours, waiting to pull a trout out with her bare hands, but Immanuel didn't have the time for that nor the patience. Instead, he took an old safety pin that had secured his ancient long johns and thanked the heaven above that he hadn't gotten a new pair. He unraveled some of the twine that held his long johns together, and taking the safety pin, he opened it up, much like a hook, got himself a longish pole from a sapling, and went to fishing.

Uzziah had fallen asleep beside the little fire Immanuel had started up, and Immanuel knew that any rest his partner could get was good rest.

———

Two hours later, he'd caught a few fish, two exactly, and was grateful to the fishing gods for allowing his little hook to work. He bent the hook back and pinned up the spot that was sagging on his long johns, then after gutting the fish, he stuck them on long sticks and cooked them.

"What's that smell, partner?" Uzziah asked.

"Fresh fish, partner, fresh trout."

Uzziah sat up and rubbed his eyes. "I actually feel a lot better."

"Then this trout should bring ya completely back to life."

They sat and ate a fish a piece, well almost. Immanuel lied about his fish. "I ain't really that hungry, ya want the rest of this one?"

Uzziah knew he was lying, but a wounded man always needs more nourishment than a whole man, so he gratefully took the other half of Immanuel's trout and blessed the Father for giving him such a generous partner.

"How far, ya reckon they are ahead of us?" Uzziah asked.

"Don't matter how far. We's gonna go after them bastards to the ends of the earth, partner. Don't care if they go to San Francisco and take a ship to Chinnie. We will follow them and kill them dead, along with any Chinnieman who gets in our way!"

That's all Uzziah wanted to hear. They weren't going to give up, and when they did find the bastards, he certainly hoped he'd be in good enough shape to participate in their demise.

Uzziah, having something in his stomach, went back to sleep there by the small fire. Immanuel didn't want to make too much smoke, otherwise they might get in more trouble with Injuns who might see the smoke. He let his partner sleep.

He wasn't sure how far those bad hombres had gone, but he knew for certain that they had no idea that someone, or someones, was actually following them. That was a good thing. They could take their time because, somewhere along the way, those hombres would think they had traveled too hard for too long, and they would settle back and relax. That's when Immanuel wanted to find them. Well, that and after he and Uzziah had procured some weapons besides a Bowie knife and a safety pin. And Uzziah needed to get better. He was headed in that healing direction, but they needed some good luck in these hard times.

3

Samuel Horatio and his daughter, Nellie, had a nice spread there with mountains on both sides. The little meadow was comfortable, and they had plenty of water, and game was abundant. Samuel had taken his wife, who was pregnant at the time, to the mountains because she had been raped, and he couldn't see staying in the town where it had happened. Besides, he wasn't sure, when she got pregnant, whether the baby was his or the bastard who had raped her.

After the baby was born, it didn't matter to either his wife, Charlotte, or himself who the father was. They simply loved Nellie, and that was it. Two years previous, about the time they had decided it was time for Nellie to be around other folks, they had figured out that it was time for them to get back to civilization. Charlotte got bit by a rattler when Samuel was out hunting that fall, and she died before he got back. Now, his beloved wife was buried next to the cabin he'd built, and he wasn't about to leave. Nellie was sixteen, and she could handle a rifle and a pistol as well as any man. They were happy being there, and that's all there was to it.

The string of men coming their way, the Poker Brothers with Francis in charge, was something that they hadn't counted on, and something that maybe the gang hadn't counted on either. Samuel was wary of just living there without any precautions, so he'd built himself and Nellie some insurance into the property they lived on. That insurance, he hoped, would be the only thing that kept them from being overrun by any gangs of bastards coming their way.

———

Francis may not have fled from trouble as many men would do, but he looked for trouble as many men would not. The Poker Brothers were left one short when Francis wanted to know what was up ahead.

"Hey, half-breed," he said, talking to the one man of the five who looked to have had mixed blood.

"Yeah, boss," Charlie Horse said. He was part Indian, and he pretended to have no idea which tribe, and his real name was some Indian name, but it wasn't Charlie Horse, but Francis liked the sound of that name, so that was what he was called. This shooter couldn't have been more than eighteen years old, and like a majority of Indians, he didn't have much facial hair, but a long braid went down his back and his hair was dark as coal.

"Scoot up ahead and find us some real good trouble to get into, maybe involving a woman or a girl, you know the kind of thing I mean."

"Sure, boss," Charlie said and rode off fast in front of them to scout out the land.

Charlie rode fast for about three hours. He had gotten way ahead of the others, then he saw a thin line of smoke that came straight from the earth and into the sky. There was no wind, so the smoke pointed right to where it was coming from. It was off down through a meadow, then back up, and down into another meadow before he saw the source of the fire. Someone was burning their fields so the soil would produce better. A good idea if you're interested in being a farmer, Charlie thought.

He turned his paint horse up on a different hill so that, when he got up there, he could look down on the place and see what was happening.

No sooner had he ground-tied the paint than he wiggled up to the top of the rise, taking off his hat first so that only his head would be exposed, then he looked down on the little farm. There was a cabin of fair size and several outbuildings that could house horses, cattle, goats, whatever one wanted in them. Chickens walked all over the place and he saw a hen house where they put them during the night. There were a couple of horses in the pasture, which had been neatly fenced off with wooden fencing, and then he saw the prize.

She was young, real young, but the bloom of womanhood was showing its pretty face, and those bumps under her shirt were bosoms, Charlie was sure. She had legs that went all the way to heaven and the blackest hair he'd seen since leaving the tribe. She wasn't no Indian though. Charlie was looking for her ma, then he spied a marker—a cross—and a hump of soil with rocks piled on it. It could be her ma's grave, or maybe her pa's, but he decided no two women would stay out there on their lonesome, and his feeling was justified when a man came from the barn and they were talking together.

Maybe it was her husband, but the way he stood away from her then kissed her on the forehead bespoke a father. He laid there a long time, watching them doing their chores, and it gave him a peaceful feeling, so peaceful that he went to sleep on that ridge. When he awakened, an hour or more had passed. They must be in the cabin because he couldn't see them anymore, and so he rode back to check in with Francis.

————————

"Did ya see the one on the hill over yonder?" Samuel Horatio asked his daughter, Nellie.

"Yeah, he was there a while, weren't he?"

"What do ya think that means, girl of mine?"

"He's scouting for someone else, or he's awful bashful," she said, and her pa laughed.

"Let's go see. I don't much cotton to people spying on me," her pa said, and the two of them saddled their horses and lit out.

————————

Charlie had stayed too long on the hill, and now, he'd have to catch up with the others and tell Francis about the young girl. He was coming up around some boulders when there in front of him was the man and the girl.

"Hold it right there, partner," the man said as he lowered a Greener and cocked both barrels.

Charlie had seen a man cut in half by a Greener and he wasn't about to make any strange moves.

"What ya doin' up this way?" the girl asked him. He liked her voice, it reminded him of a raven who could talk, sort of rough and smooth at the same time.

"Saw yer smoke, curious, that's all," Charlie said.

"I'm Samuel Horatio," the man said, "and that there's my daughter, Nellie."

"Charlie Horse," he said, knowing how stupid it sounded.

Both the man and his daughter looked at each other, but neither of them laughed.

"That yer real name, Charlie Horse?" Nellie asked him politely.

"Well, yeah, guess my old man thought it was funny or something."

"Yer comin' back with us," the father of the girl said.

"Why?"

"Just in case," the girl said.

In case of what, Charlie wondered, but he didn't have much choice in the matter with that Greener on him.

They rode in the back of him and his back itched thinking of all that buckshot hitting him from behind. When they got back to the ranch, they put their horses up, and Charlie tied his paint to the hitching post out front of the cabin.

"Come on inside," the man said, and he did so.

When he was seated at the big wooden table, he saw the girl put hobbles on the paint, both front and back. *Guess they don't want me going nowhere.*

Nellie, the young girl, fried chicken. Charlie could remember seeing a chicken coop out back of the house, and he reckoned there was one less chicken out there.

After supper, in which no one had said a word, the man spoke up.

"Want coffee?"

He did and he nodded so.

The girl poured the coffee from the pot in the fire-place, which must have been made this morning because you could probably stand a spoon in it. But it tasted good, especially with the cream from the cow and some sugar in it.

"Am I a prisoner?" Charlie asked the both of them.

"No, but ya can't leave just yet," Samuel said.

"Why not, I got places to be."

"Like where?" Nellie asked the half-breed.

He didn't answer, not only because he didn't want to tell them about Francis Grossman and the other boys, but because this was America and it was none of their business.

"Got us a silent one," Samuel Horatio said and laughed. The girl laughed, too, and he didn't like the way their laughter sounded.

"You ain't the first one to wander in here," the girl said.

"Oh yeah?"

"Yeah," her pa said.

"Who were the others?" he asked.

"No one you'd know," Nellie said, and both she and her pa laughed about that.

He still had his gun strapped to his thigh, and if that Greener hadn't been balanced on the table and pointing in his direction, Charlie imagined he might kill the old man. Well, he wasn't that old, but kill the pa and take what he wanted from the raven-headed girl. She was woman enough for him, and he'd probably be the first, unless of course, her pa had tasted it.

"Well, like I said, I got places to be," Charlie said and looked between the two of them.

"You'll leave in the mornin'," Samuel said, then added, "and that's that!"

———

They tied him up and set him next to the fireplace so, they claimed, he wouldn't get cold.

"It can get cold up this high," Nellie said, "So, be grateful, we ain't somebody who'd take advantage."

This was the first time Charlie had ever been scared of a sixteen-year-old girl and her pa, and he chastised himself for thinking such stupid thoughts. What in the world could a slip of a girl and her pa do to him, a full-grown man?

The man made sure the tying up was good and pushed him closer to the low fire, and sure enough, it was getting cold outside. He fell asleep and was awakened by the girl who was standing over him. She was young and perfectly made, and her perky little bosoms sat right up and begged to be handled underneath her chemise.

"Ain't been many young men up this way in some time," she whispered in her raven voice.

"That a fact," he whispered back.

"Yes, it is. Ya sure ya got someplace to be? My pa could give ya chores, and we got sort of a bunk house back there," she said and pointed.

"And if I was to stay, what then?"

"Well," she said, coming closer and sitting on the floor beside him.

"Ya got nice hair."

"Not as nice as yours, little girlie," he said.

"I ain't that little," she said, sitting back and batting her eyelashes at him. "I could probably like you," she added, lifting her chin to look into his eyes.

"I'd like to see more of ya," he said as he looked down at her chest.

"Ya would, would ya?"

"Acourse."

"You ask my pa ifn ya can stay and help us out around here. That way," she said, standing back up, "you could see more of me, understand? Like normal people, we could learn what each likes and how the sun shines on us as people."

"You mean settle down here?"

"Maybe, maybe not?"

"Why ya teasin' me?"

"I ain't doin' nothin' but talking to ya in the middle of the night, that ain't teasin' is it," she said as she stood and started to walk away.

"Untie me."

"That ain't gonna happen."

"Don't yaw wanna be with me?"

"Maybe, maybe not." she said and walked back into one of the back rooms.

————

In the morning, they fixed breakfast, and while he was

eating, he kept looking at the girl and wondering what the hell she was up to.

"I don't care much fer ya lookin' at my daughter like that," Samuel said.

"Sorry, boss, she's just such a good cook. Hard to believe ya taught her all this."

"I didn't," he said and left it at that.

When they were through and the dishes had been done, they gave him back his pistol, which he hadn't missed until they handed it back to him. Not like him to not miss his gun. He could see that it wasn't loaded, and the gun belt had no shells in it.

"How am I supposed to get by without no bullets?" he asked the both of them.

She held up a gunny sack.

"They're in there?" he asked, and she nodded *yes*.

They rode him out to the road, well, it was a game trail, really, and handed him the sack. Nellie had blindfolded him before they left the little ranch, and with it all black before his eyes, all he could think about was her teasing him like she did that night. Maybe he should stay.

"I'm a good worker. I could stay if ya liked?" he said to the man.

The man looked between his daughter, who seemed not to be able to keep her eyes off him.

"I think not," he said, and Charlie could feel the expression on Nellie's face drop. So much for him staying on and possibly getting a poke.

They rode for a couple hours, but he could tell, he had a great sense of direction, that they were turning back and back, so he doubted they'd gone very far from the little ranch.

"I'm gonna be nearby for a spell, ifn ya take the blindfold off afore I'm ready fer ya to, I'll kill ya, understand?" the man said.

He understood all right. He sat that horse, that paint, for the better part of an hour. His paint had dozed off and was hip shot and drowsy when he decided to finally take off the blindfold. He thought about taking it off a couple times, but then thought better of it. How did he know that man, Samuel, could be sitting right there with his Greener trained on him? He'd heard them ride off, but people can sneak back, even people who ain't Indians. When he finally tore off the blindfold, they were nowhere to be seen.

When he got to where he recognized a place he'd been, he took off up the way to see if he could find Francis Grossman and the other four Poker Brothers. It was nearly nightfall when he spotted their trail, and boy was he glad. He just wanted to get back to some people whom he knew.

———

"Where the hell you been?" Francis asked as he threw a right leg over and hooked it around the saddle horn. He had a habit of sitting like that on a still horse. He lit a small cigar and smoked while he waited for Charlie to spit it out.

And spit it out, he did. He told them about finding the place, spying on the old man and his son, then about falling asleep, and them catching him and taking him home. He thought about telling them about the sixteen-year-old girl, but hell, it was too good a story to tell these washed-out saddle tramps.

They all drifted off at different times, but as Charlie was about to leave for the happy sleeping grounds, he rolled over and saw Jeremiah Bills, whose eyes were wide open. He was rumored to be a preacher's boy. Jeremiah had the face of an angel and could fight 'til the sun came up, but he rarely got involved in any discussions around the fire.

"What'd ya leave out?" Jeremiah whispered to Charlie.

"What d'ya mean?" Charlie whispered back.

"There's more to the story than ya told, ain't there?"

Charlie scooted closer to where Jeremiah was rolled up in his blankets.

"Ya promise not to tell?"

"On the Bible," the preacher's boy said.

"Well, there was this young thing, musta been sixteen or seventeen maybe. She had one of them athletic bodies like women who ride horses a lot."

"Oh yeah?" Jeremiah's eyes got bigger.

"Yeah, she came out and flirted with me, asked me to stay on."

"No."

"Yeah, then afore she left me tied up there in front of the fire, she unbuttoned her shirt, and I could see all the way to her navel," Charlie lied just for the hell of it.

"Oh my God!"

"I asked her why she was teasin' me so, and she said she might tease me even more ifn I stayed to help her pa."

"Why didn't ya?"

"Her pa weren't too hot on the idea in the morning."

"Hey guys!" Jeremiah yelled, and all the guys yelled back for him to shut his trap.

"Ya gonna wanna hear this," Jeremiah said, and with Charlie thinking all the while that he should never have trusted no preacher's kid, Jeremiah rolled out the entire story but told 'em she had taken off her clothes and rubbed herself against Charlie as he was tied up.

"Oh my God!" Terry Pearsall yelled, "We gotta go back and help that girl outta her virginity, right!"

A rousing cheer went up from everyone around the fire and no one was asleep anymore.

Everyone laughed, and Francis watched them, then spoke.

"First thing we got to do is kick the living shite out of this Injun boy for lying to us!"

Charlie Horse looked around at what he had thought were his friends. They all got up as one body and moved toward him. He looked over to where the paint was tied along the high line and made a break for the horse.

On the way there, somebody tackled him and they went down in a clutter of dust, then there was nothing but pain.

They kicked him, punched him, tore at his clothes, and it might have taken no more than five minutes, but by the time they all wandered away to their bedrolls, Charlie Horse was a bleeding mess. He limped back to where his saddle and bedroll were. Francis looked at him when he passed by.

"Let that be a lesson to you, boy. When men are together there aren't any secrets, you understand?"

Charlie just looked at Francis like he wanted to kill him.

Francis took his Winchester and threw the butt of it into Charlie's stomach. He grunted, then bending over, he vomited up everything he'd eaten at supper.

"In the morning, we'll go find the ranch, kill the farmer, and have at his young daughter, then will everyone be satisfied?"

"We need to draw lots," Bill said.

"What fer? Ifn she's that young ain't gonna matter when ya have a go at her, will it?" Terry asked.

"I don't like used quim, especially right after it's been used, ifn ya know what I mean," Bill explained himself.

"First come, first served," Manson Quills said. Manson was a small man who had a bad temper. He was good at cards, liked to mess with people, but had a mean streak in him a mile wide.

"Well, boys, what do you think?" Francis asked in his perfect English.

Everybody wanted to talk at the same time, and by the time he shut them all up, he said, "Sounds to me like each and every one of you wants a taste of that young girl. Am I right?"

"Boss, can I say something here?" Charlie asked politely from his bleeding position on the ground.

"Sure, go ahead, Charlie."

"Hey, I probably should have told ya about the girl. After the beating ya just gave me, I know I shoulda told ya, but there's something strange about her pa and her, and I can't put my finger on it—"

"But I betcha wish ya could!" interrupted Bill Mathers, a big portly man who looked younger 'cause his face, stretched out by all his fat, didn't have any wrinkles.

"What ifn I go scout out the ranch again and help all of you find it?" Charlie asked.

"Just how stupid do ya think we are, half-breed?" Terry Pearsall said. Terry was the shortest man that Francis had ever seen without being a midget.

"We ain't all short on body and brains!" Manson quipped as he stood up next to Terry, showing how short the man was.

"Whoa! Whoa! All of you had better settle down," Francis said, realizing that this young quim was about to tear apart his recently organized gang.

"What's your take on this, Jeremiah?" Francis asked.

"Don't want no part in it," Jeremiah said and left it at that and yet he was the one who had told all the rest of them. Maybe he was jealous about the real story that Charlie had told him, who knew?

"Good, that means there'll be more fer the rest of us," Manson said.

"Okay, okay, doesn't sound like we're going to make any money on this, gentlemen, but there is the factors of amusement and entertainment, which surely gets my attention," Francis added.

"Ya gonna have some of that new quim?" Terry asked the boss.

"Not interested. I like women, who know what they're doing, and rape has always seemed rather too primitive for my tastes."

4

Uzziah was actually looking better, or so Immanuel thought. Perhaps some of the plants he'd harvested along the way and boiled up and put on the wound were doing his partner some good. They were still tracking the six men who had shot Uzziah and knocked Immanuel out, and the trail was pristine as no rain had fallen in the past week.

Immanuel felt they were getting closer, but he had no real way of telling. He just felt it in his bones. It was almost as if the group of six bad hombres had doubled back and were coming their way. That's when Immanuel saw the smoke. It was lazy and coming straight up off the fire, and giving just about anybody the position of where that fire was. They walked right up to the small ranch and there didn't seem to be anyone home. The fire was a bunch of brush that someone had gathered and set ablaze. Immanuel saw the horses in the corral and the cow and chickens, and you'd have thought he'd just entered Saint Louis, except they were wanted there, and they were both glad it wasn't.

"Where do ya suppose they's got off to, Uzziah?"

He was sitting on the donkey and weary as hell. Even though Immanuel kept telling him he was looking better, he really didn't feel much better.

"Got no idea, partner, let's sit on the porch and wait fer them to come back," Uzziah said as he dismounted the donkey, walked up the few steps to the porch, and sat down in the first rocker he came to.

Immanuel was looking all around when he saw the grave.

"Well, somebody's died up this way, that's fer sure," and he pointed to the rock-covered grave.

They hadn't stopped during the night and both of them were tired, especially Immanuel, who had walked all the way. Immanuel tied the donkey to the hitching post and both men came up and sat on the rockers. They had finally reached some sort of civilization and both were relieved. They rocked for a bit, then both men were asleep.

———

When Nellie and her pa, Samuel, rode up, they were a bit amazed. Samuel had left the brush burning but had dug a trench around it, and it was far enough away from other brush and burned down enough that he hadn't worried about it spreading. What they saw first was the donkey tied to their hitching post, then two men, big men, sitting in their rockers, and both of them sleeping.

The way they were dressed was a bit comical. They

looked like grown men dressed in children's clothes. Their pants were held up by rope and the end of their pants were halfway up their calves. The shirts they wore had the sleeves cut off, and even that hadn't stopped the shirts from ripping around their massive arms. One of them had been injured and had bandages on his right shoulder, the other didn't seem harmed. As far as Samuel could tell, there was one weapon between the two of them—a Bowie knife. Seriously, there couldn't be hidden on their persons any other weapons, there simply wasn't room.

"What do ya make of this, Nellie girl?" her pa asked her before they dismounted.

"Pa, I ain't seen anything as pathetic for some time."

Just then, it must have been the sounds of their voices, Immanuel awoke and grabbed the Bowie knife. Even though that was the only weapon they obviously had, Samuel was concerned for his daughter.

"Don't make any quick moves, mister," he said, lowering the Greener on Immanuel.

"Thank God you're here," Immanuel said.

———

Uzziah was brought into the house and put in the spare bed. Well, Nellie's ma and pa had counted on having other children before she died of that snake bite. Uzziah kept saying over and over again how grateful he was before he finally fell into a deep sleep. The man was exhausted.

Immanuel got some clothes from Samuel. He wasn't as big as Immanuel, but he was a whole heap closer in size than the dead old timer they'd found.

Immanuel regaled them with the story of the wedding and what had happened when they left. How they had been bushwhacked and everything taken from them. Told them about the knife tied to his leg beneath the union suit and how he had boiled water in bark and made the medicines that had partially cured his partner, Uzziah. They could hear Uzziah talking in his sleep in the other room. He wasn't making any sense whatsoever.

"Don't mind him, the man talks all the time, even when he's sleeping."

He went on to tell Nellie and her pa where they lived way up in the Rockies and just about everything about them, but not how they had killed that undersheriff who had killed the woman they had both cared about. Information like that just wasn't shared. But every Westerner knew that other Westerners had done what was necessary to survive, and some of that was privileged information.

Finally, Nellie cooked supper, and they woke Uzziah up and were at the table about to eat the turkey that Samuel had shot, when Uzziah spoke up.

"Mind if I bless the food?"

They didn't.

"Heavenly Father, we give thanks not only for this repast which we are about to partake of, but fer these good folks who have willingly, or unwillingly, taken us in. Thank you, Father, for the generous spirits of those who live out west, and bless these folks and let them prosper. In Jesus's name, and everybody said, Amen."

Uzziah and Immanuel ate as if they hadn't eaten in weeks, and truth be told, it sure felt that way. It was a good thing that a turkey had been killed because, between Samuel, his daughter, and the two mountain men, they nearly finished the entire bird. There were spuds, greens, and even a cake that Nellie had made. Uzziah couldn't tell exactly what kind of cake it was, it wasn't vanilla and it wasn't chocolate.

"What kinda cake is this?" he asked Nellie.

"Elderberry."

"Well, I'll be, who knew?"

"Ifn ya put enough sugar with it, just about any cake will taste good," she said smiling.

———

Charlie knew exactly where Samuel Horatio and his daughter, Nellie, lived, but he was taking the gang the long way around. He had strange thoughts about the girl, and the thought of the gang just rolling in and having their way with her made his heart ache. He had never felt that way about any gal and thought maybe, just maybe, there might be something there. The second night they camped on the way to the little ranch house, Francis spoke up.

"Charlie, I like you, but you had better find this place you were telling us about tomorrow, or else. You understand?"

Charlie understood all right. The rest of the gang had thoughts about young girls on their minds and they didn't take kindly to being led around by the nose and not finding that quim.

In the early morning hours, Charlie woke up. He still hurt like hell from the beating he'd taken a couple of nights ago. Leaving his bedding behind like he had gone into the woods to do some business, he made his way toward his paint. On the way there, one of the Hawkens was leaning against a tree. He picked it up. That beating had to be worth something. He got to his horse. It wasn't saddled, but what did that matter to an Indian? He slipped up on him, and without making a sound, the two of them walked right out of the camp.

Once he'd cleared the camp, he made a beeline for the little ranch but took caution enough, for some of the men could track all right, but none of them could track like Charlie. He was fairly sure they might find the place, but not before he got back to Nellie and warned her and her pa what was coming their way. He rode for nearly two days before he knew he was coming close to the girl who had bothered him so, and for whom he had taken not only a sizable shine to, but also a beating.

———

"Rider comin' fast!" Uzziah said from the front porch. Nellie was in the kitchen cleaning up the breakfast mess, and her pa and Immanuel had gone after game.

She came out of the kitchen with the Greener in her hands, and to Uzziah, it looked like she knew how to use it. Off in the distance, coming from the meadow, they could see dust rising up. For sure, someone was riding hard toward them.

"Got any idea who this might be?" Uzziah asked.

"None whatsoever," she said, but in her heart of hearts, she was hoping, had been hoping since Charlie left, that he just might come back, for she had surely teased him bad enough, and she did know what men wanted, her pa had warned her often enough, and if she'd done her job right, this just might be him.

Uzziah got the spyglass out and was focusing in on the rider, who was visible now from far away.

"It's a cowboy, but he's ridin' bareback like an Injun, and he ain't wasting no time."

"Let me see," she said and, taking the spyglass, looked at the rider through it. It was Charlie, and she was so glad that it was him, and that her pa was away when he'd decided to come back. "I know this man," she said and left it at that.

Charlie rode in hard, and when he put the brakes on the paint, the horse slid to a stop. *It was a neat bit of riding,* Uzziah thought.

Whomever the boy was, he'd been beaten pretty bad. It had happened a few days ago because a lot of the beating had scabbed over, but there were spots that still bled.

———

The minute Charlie was off his horse and running for Nellie's arms, he recognized the stranger sitting on the porch. He was one of two mountain men that the Poker Brothers, under Francis Grossman, had waylaid not long after they'd gotten together. In fact, one of the Hawkens which they had taken from the men, he was now carrying in his hand. He had left without his saddle but had considered it bad form not to take the long rifle with him.

———

Uzziah recognized his own weapon, and he sat up in the rocker and couldn't wait to hear the rest of this Indian's story. He looked and the bareback horse, the paint, which the man had ridden in on, was shod, just as the six horses ridden by the men who had jumped them.

The Indian and Nellie embraced even though he was a virtual stranger to her, and she, him. Something had happened that night when she teased him that had sparked a connection between them. Neither of them understood any more than anyone understood what love does when it hits people.

"What happened to you, Charlie?" Nellie asked when she broke from the hug. Did ya fall off yer paint?"

"There ain't a horse alive that could buck me offa him," Charlie bragged.

Uzziah heard the brag and knew that the half-breed had not had a chance on Shadow.

They didn't kiss, that would have to wait 'til later. They hugged again, and this time, Nellie was a bit more maternal in the way she held him. As they broke from the hug, Charlie spoke.

"They're comin' fer ya," he said, his breath still not caught after riding a hard way fast.

"Who?"

"The men I was ridin' with, they're comin' fer ya," Charlie repeated.

Uzziah had decided he would keep his mouth closed 'til Immanuel and Samuel made their way back with the game. But he sure wished he had a gun on him.

"Come up on the porch and let's talk," Nellie said, thinking that he was being awful mysterious about men coming for her.

Charlie started up on the porch, and having recognized Uzziah right away, he decided to play it as coy as he could.

Up there on the porch, one eye on Nellie and the other on Uzziah, Charlie told his sordid tale. Even the part about not wanting to tell the gang but telling Jeremiah, the preacher's kid, because he thought maybe the boy could keep a secret. He knew better now. *Never trust a preacher's kid* was his motto now. When he'd finished his tale, he took a long look at Uzziah. He knew the two men they bushwhacked had not seen anything —certainly he, Charlie, had not been seen by either of the men, but the Hawken he carried from their camp, well, the mountain man must have recognized it, he was sure of that. But still, he wasn't sure, he thought he'd test the man.

"Don't I know you?" he asked Uzziah.

Fool me once, shame on you, fool me twice, shame on me, Uzziah thought.

"My partner and I was bushwhacked a while back, and when I got shot, I fell off my horse and hit my head, hell, stranger, we might know one another, but besides knowing my own name and where I come from, I couldn't tell ya much about the last couple weeks," Uzziah lied, looking at the half-breed, he thought the boy just might have believed him. It would be a different story when Immanuel got there, he was just as likely to start shooting at the young man as he was to greet him, especially once he'd seen the Hawken rifle he was carrying.

Nellie got Charlie a cup of coffee, and the three of them sat on the porch, Charlie drinking his coffee and Uzziah keeping an eye on the Indian 'til they heard the sound of approaching horses. Nellie jumped up, holding the Greener like she was ready to use it.

"Could that be them?" she asked Charlie, turning her head in his direction.

"Nah, I didn't get them anywheres near here, and I certainly didn't leave 'em any trail to follow."

As Samuel and Immanuel rode up, both men drew their weapons. Samuel had found an old pistol he no longer used and let Immanuel strap it on, and both carried Winchester rifles. On the back of each horse was a dead deer, the hunt had been successful. That was good.

"What the hell ya doin' here, boy!?" Samuel asked Charlie, "Didn't we send ya on yer way a while back?"

"Pa, he's got some bad news, there's a gang of men comin' this way to take me," Nellie blurted out.

"What!?" Samuel exclaimed.

For the second time, Uzziah sat as Nellie and Charlie went through the story of the gang, how Charlie had inadvertently told them of the girl, and how now they were coming for her. The whole time this was going on, Uzziah and Immanuel were exchanging glances dealing with the Hawken the boy had brought with him and the fact that Charlie was probably from the gang of six the two mountain men had been attacked by.

Immanuel went over and checked the hoof prints of the boy's paint, and sure enough, he nodded to Uzziah that it was, in fact, one of the six horses that had been in on the attack. Hoof prints might seem like generic nothings to just about anybody, but when you have been around horses all your life and you're a tracker, they might as well be a picture of the horse who made them.

No two horses rode the same way, and no two horses wore their shoes the same.

The conversation about the gang and what they were up to stopped abruptly as Immanuel walked up behind the Indian and cocked the pistol that Samuel had lent him.

"What are you doin'?" Nellie wanted to know.

"This here man is one part of the gang that attacked me and my partner. This here may be a trick, they could be layin' out there right now, waitin' fer us to relax, and then they will move on in," Immanuel announced.

"Why you no-good half-breed," Samuel started in, cocking his Winchester and aiming at the middle of Charlie's chest.

"Wait a minute, Pa, we been here for a couple hours afore ya showed back up with the game. Would they have waited fer more men to come before they took us by surprise?" she asked, looking between the two men.

Immanuel and Samuel looked at each other. Actually, his daughter had made a lot of sense. If a group of men wanted to attack a hurt man, a girl, and a young boy, they would not have waited for reinforcements to show.

"What ya think, mountain man?" Samuel asked Immanuel. People just trusted Immanuel, that's all there was to it. When problems arose, they looked to him, and Uzziah knew why. He was smart and had stayed alone in the mountains for a long time, and you didn't do that being stupid.

"I think yer daughter's right. They ain't near here, and ifn what Charlie says is correct, then it might take them a time to get here, but I can tell ya this. Ifn they got the notion that there's a purty girl in these here foothills, and she is unguarded except fer her pa, well, they'll be riding for her, that's a fact."

"Well, I guess that means we gotta prepare a welcoming committee fer these gents," Samuel mysteriously said, and the two mountain men just looked at each other.

5

Samuel Horatio was a smart man. He knew that living all this way out away from people was going to cause some men, and certainly some Indians, to think that he was vulnerable. In his imagination, before they had arrived where they settled, he had drawn up plans for what to do with a place that wasn't around a lot of other folks. Immanuel and Uzziah weren't about to ask the man why he didn't want to live around others, because that was the same situation they were in, and they certainly weren't going to reveal to total strangers what they had done to the undersheriff.

When Samuel, his wife, and their baby girl, Nellie, arrived at the spot that Samuel knew was their home, he drew up the plans which he had in his mind. It was these plans which he took from a tube of cardboard and, pulling them out, stretched them on the big wooden table inside the cabin. Salt, pepper, sugar, and sorghum held the four corners down.

Everybody looked down on these drawings, but hardly anyone knew what they meant.

"These here plans are my security blanket in times of trouble," Samuel said.

"Now," Immanuel began, "are these things ya wanted to do, or things ya actually done?"

It was a good question. Uzziah could read plans a bit, and he saw a lot of work that would have been hard for one man, a wife, and a little girl to accomplish.

"I got a lot of it done, but there's a lot that ain't done neither," Samuel said, then started explaining the plans.

"These here lines that are broken and continue on are actually tunnels which I dug. The earth here is good, and with the support of beams, I made a tunnel from under the kitchen all the way out to that there tree line," he said, pointing out the window toward the north. "I had planned on digging another tunnel from the bedrooms but never got around to it. This here," he said, pointing to a set of double lines that ran along one side of the settlement. "This here is a ditch which is covered by boards and can be rode over, but ifn we need it, it could be a line of defense. I mean ifn ya put a man in that ditch with a rifle, he could create a lot of havoc for anybody comin' in from that direction. And over here," he said, pointing inside the tree line. "I have installed a couple of weighted down what-ya-call-em? It's like that medieval weapon which has all the points coming from a ball?"

"Yeah, that's a mace," Uzziah chimed in.

"Yeah, that's what I thought. Anyways, these maces are tied back in the trees, which are along two trails that lead into this compound. Ifn those ropes are cut at just the right time, they swing out over the trail and wipe out anything in their way."

"Damn, young son," Immanuel began, "ya got a veritable fort here, don't ya?"

"Well, each of these tricks, as I call 'em, only works once, then there's no surprise."

"But still, with only five men coming at us, how many times do they hafta work?" Uzziah commented.

6

The boy who called himself Charlie Horse came from a tribe of Indians that wasn't that far away. They were known as the Chippewa Cree nation. They lived mostly in eastern Montana territory, and each year, they lost more and more young boys to the ways of the White man. A small band had come down off the Montana territory and was looking for Stone Child, which was Charlie's real name. He was the grandson of one of the medicine men of the tribe and had wandered away when he saw a wagon train going through south of where they lived.

He was only seventeen at the time but was tired of the Indian ways, and because he had the second sight from his grandfather, the medicine man, he could see the writing on the wall. The White men would keep coming and be like the sand at the lake. They were too numerous to fight and too many to forget. Stone Child had a strong urge to be a warrior, but the medicine he'd been taught and the medicine he had was a medicine of peace. Members of his tribe tried to fit in wherever they could, and Stone Child had decided he wanted to fit in with the Whites. They had all the towns, and money. It was a win-win situation for the boy. He had to leave his squaw behind, but he could always find another one.

He had been fortunate that someone in the wagon train had taken him in and hid him from the others, and when they got to where they were going, Stone Child ran away. He cleaned spittoons in saloons and lived in back rooms until he had enough money to buy a gun, and as far as he was concerned, that gun was his passage into the White man's world. He practiced every day and learned how to play poker, and wasn't bad at it because he had a sixth sense of what the other fellas at the table were holding.

It wasn't like he knew the cards they held. It was only that when he looked in their faces, he knew if they thought they could win or not. He had made a bit of money when he sat at the table in that bar where Francis Grossman showed up. He only knew those men because he drifted into town and they played poker a lot.

And yet his grandfather, who wasn't that old, wanted his grandson Stone Child back. He missed the boy who had been more like him as a youth than his father had been. The small band of Chippewa Cree that traveled down the Rockies in search of Stone Child was led by the grandfather, and from time to time, the old man would pretend to be a drunken Indian and wander into towns and listen to what the White man was saying. One day about two weeks ago, in that disguise, he'd heard the story of the half-breed boy who was playing poker when a fight broke out between a White man named Francis Grossman and the sheriff and another man at the bar, for some reason all those he was playing cards with had gotten involved and rode out of town with the man Grossman, who had essentially started the fight.

When he left the bar, he joined back up with the other Chippewa Cree and followed them to where the two mountain men were robbed and everything they owned was taken. Stone Child's grandfather had to hold the others from helping the two stranded White men. He wanted to see what they were made of and if they would survive. It was a test of both bravery and cunning. He liked the biggest of the men who hadn't been shot. The man knew plants and was able, through a lot of skills, to bring his friend back from the brink of death. To Stone Child's grandfather, this man was a medicine man within the world of the White man.

Men who terrorize other men never think that they might be followed by other kinder, gentler men. So, it was with Stone Child. He kept on with the five other bad men, but his grandfather knew that he was a good boy. If only he could get him back, then everything would be all right with the small band of Cree up in the Montana territory, but Stone Child's grandfather was smart. He knew that simply taking the boy back against his will wasn't going to work. It would have to be Stone Child's will to come back, which would ensure that he would stay with the small band of Cree.

And so it was that Stone Child's grandfather and the other Cree watched as the two men, who had been ambushed, made their way to where Stone Child had been held captive for one night. The man and the girl who lived at the small ranch were good people and only wanted to be left alone, but in a world of violence, it was rare for someone to walk that path with success.

They watched as the two men who were regaining their strength and the man and girl, along with Stone Child, gathered together as a band against the bad men who were coming their way. Stone Child's grandfather had seen the many tricks and hidden dangers that the man and girl had built to help keep them safe, and it amused him. He and the small band of Chippewa Cree would stay and watch to see if the good would overcome the bad, and if and when it was necessary, they might swoop down, but only after they had seen if Stone Child's medicine would be able to fight for the good and kill the bad men who were coming.

———

Stone Child, known in the White man's world as Charlie Horse, stood in the early morning mist that had come up from the creek running through the meadow. The girl reminded him of someone he had known when he was little, he wasn't sure who, but he knew that it had been a woman in the tribe. He stood and looked into the surrounding hills. He felt that the Great Spirit was watching over him even now. It was a tribal custom to be generous and giving. The medicine men, like his grandfather, believed generosity was the source of all the good things that came into their lives.

They valued the sweet grass which grew along the banks of rivers and streams. Stone Child, Charlie Horse, walked down by the creek and there was a lot of sweet grass growing there. He gathered up a bunch and sang a little song his grandfather had taught him. He wasn't sure now what all the words were, but he knew it was about keeping clean and being able to leave this earth whenever he was called without regretting anything in his past. That's the way the Chippewa Cree were taught. He was dressed that morning only in his jeans and hat. He felt more like himself when he didn't wear a shirt.

As he was coming up from the little stream, he saw the girl, Nellie, her pa called her. She saw him, and instead of speaking, she wandered down to where he was. She saw the handful of sweetgrass that he'd gathered, and she, too, began picking it. They went along the side of the creek that he hadn't covered, and together, they grabbed a lot of sweetgrass.

———

Stone Child's grandfather liked the girl immediately. She had the hair of his own mother and was, in fact, a striking resemblance of the woman. Perhaps it was the Great Spirit that had brought Stone Child to this young girl so that he could reclaim his heritage. Sometimes, it took going to the way outside the way to find the way back inside the way. He and his small band of Chippewa Cree were camped not far away, and Stone Child's grandfather knew that the battle that was to come would determine the fate of Stone Child and the young girl.

———

Samuel showed Immanuel and Uzziah exactly where he'd placed the maces and the hidden places where riflemen could jump out of and cause a lot of trouble for whoever wanted to gain entrance to the little meadow where he and Nellie lived. The trouble with the maces was that someone had to be there to cut the ropes that would send them traveling fast across the trails they were meant to protect. And there were only four of them. True, four against five wasn't bad odds, but still, it meant whoever was behind the ride who got swept away by the mace would have a clear shot at the man who had cut the rope.

Uzziah and Immanuel talked long into the night about how they could best handle the situation.

"They won't be ridin' Shadow, that's a fer sure," Uzziah said to Immanuel. They had taken to sleeping out on the porch. It wasn't that cold, wrapping up in blankets that Nellie brought them. They could smoke and watch the night, which was exactly what they needed to do.

"No, but they'll bring Shadow along because he's too valuable to leave behind," Immanuel said as he sipped from the cup of coffee with a shot of whiskey in it.

"True. I just hope they don't get so frustrated with Shadow that they think he's a pain in the butt and kill him," Uzziah said, pouring some of that same whiskey that Samuel had brought out to them.

"They'll never kill Shadow. Is that his name?" It was Charlie. His wounds had begun to heal.

The two mountain men looked at the Indian boy who had been with the men who attacked them.

"So, now yer gonna tell us how ya tried to stop them from hurting us, is that right?" Uzziah said, still mad as hell about being shot.

"Nah, I won't lie to you two. I was with 'em, and I was the one of the ones who stripped ya down."

"Well," Immanuel said, "at least he ain't pretendin' he wasn't there."

"It was my tomahawk that brought you down," Charlie admitted.

"Why you—" Immanuel started in.

"It weren't no accident that it was the blunt end which gotcha. I coulda thrown it different and yer brains would be back there."

Immanuel cooled down. If the boy was right, then he was glad he'd thrown it the way he had.

"I heard ya tell the gal there that there weren't no horse ya couldn't ride. Did ya ride Shadow?" Uzziah asked, wondering if his horse had been broken by another man.

"Nah, after three of them got bucked off, they wouldn't give me a chance. But I heard Francis tell one of the guys that he knew a buyer who would give plenty for the horse."

———

Francis was getting tired of riding. He'd checked his cash and realized what they really needed before attacking a man and his pretty daughter was some change in their pockets and some whiskey. They were going to need whiskey when they saw what Francis was going to do to the girl. After they finished with her, he planned on burning her at the stake while her father watched. He'd done that once before, and it made him want to do it again. He especially liked the way human flesh smelled when it was on fire. It reminded him of smoking hams back home.

"Hey, we are going to take a side trip here, gents," he announced on the third morning of their search for the meadow with the cabin and the pretty girl.

"Come on, boss, everybody's looking forward to some fun," Terry Pearsall said.

"Yeah, but wouldn't it be more fun with whiskey?" Francis asked, knowing they would all agree. "And maybe our pockets stuffed with cash?"

That got the group's attention!

They rode for a small town that Francis knew was nestled up in the hills not far from where they were. Hell, there was a sawmill there which was fat once a month with the payroll of a timber baron who was denuding the hills around the town at great profit. So, what if they had to take a little detour before coming back and having some fun. They'd rob the payroll from the sawmill and then find the girl and her pa and have even more fun. Francis could already smell the flesh burning, and it was pleasant—like a good old-fashioned barbeque.

They rode for two days away from where they had originally planned to go, and when they rode into the town of Wiesnerville, they were ready for whiskey and the saloon. Hitching all their horses, plus Shadow, out in front of the saloon, they went in and started drinking.

Francis pulled the barkeep aside.

"Say, do you know a man name Wiesner who lives around here?"

"Yeah, of course, he's the man who owns the sawmill."

"Where would I find him, this time of day?"

The barkeep looked up at the big clock on the opposite wall.

"He'll still be up at the mill," he said and continued wiping the bar with his dirty rag.

Francis made sure his four men had enough cash to enjoy themselves and told them he was going to see a man about a horse. They took the extra cash for drinking and whoring and didn't mind that Francis left the saloon.

Back outside, Francis looked the black stallion over. He was one beautiful horse, and even if he couldn't be ridden, he knew that the man he was going to see would pay high dollar for a stud horse. He had known Joe Wiesner back in the day when he was a respectable citizen and they had attended the synagogue where Francis's father was the rabbi. He looked forward to robbing the man blind, then slitting his throat. Joe had always been one sanctimonious son of a bitch, and he wondered if Joe's God would save him from the hell to come.

7

They had waited a long time for the rest of this gang to show, and if Uzziah and Immanuel hadn't known for sure that they had been robbed blind by the six men, they would have been on their way. But mountain men had a code, and part of that unwritten code was they would never, ever leave anyone in the lurch if they could help it, themselves included.

The two of them went out to check the defensive positions again that Samuel had built. This time, they had gone without him.

"Whatcha think?" Uzziah asked Immanuel as they were standing on the trail that had one of the maces on it.

"Well, first of all, there's not really a good place to hide. I mean, if someone was comin' down the trail and ridin' fast, okay, maybe they wouldn't see ya, but if they were sneakin', they'd look up and wonder, *Why's that person standing beside that tree, and oh yeah, what's that bunch of stuff wrapped together tied to the tree?*"

Uzziah had stayed down on the trail and he could hear Immanuel without any problem, but then again, Uzziah had the hearing of a much younger man. Uzziah looked to Immanuel as if he were healing well. Once Immanuel'd properly boiled up some of the remedies he'd found in the area, they'd worked wonders on Uzziah's health. He gained a bit of weight back and looked like he might be able to handle himself in a fight. When the fighting did begin, however, Immanuel was going to make sure it was Uzziah who had the Hawken. They were both excellent shots, but he didn't want his weakened partner wrestling around with someone who—at this point—might be too much for him.

"I agree," Uzziah yelled up to Immanuel, "these so-called fortifications risk yer life as much as they save it."

———

Francis could see where the smoke from the mill was rising, He mounted up his horse, and taking the lead rope for the big black stallion, he rode toward the smoke. It took him less than an hour to get there. The mill hired a lot of the local folks, but they didn't want all that smoke in town. When he got there, he could see what must be the office over against a denuded hill. He rode over, tied both the horses up, walked the eight steps to the office, and simply walked in.

The man at the desk, Joseph Wiesner, looked up. It took him a second, then he recognized the man standing in his office.

"Grossman, my God," he said as he got up and rounded the end of the desk he'd been sitting at, and the two men shook hands. "Where in the hell have you been?"

"Causing trouble here and there."

"No doubt. What in the world are you doing up this way? You trying to get a minyan together?" he asked, referring to the synagogal requirement of gathering ten Jewish men for certain religious ceremonies.

"Hell, I ain't been in a synagogue since I walked out that day I had the argument with my old man."

"Me neither, I mean, not since I moved out here. It ain't like there's a bunch of Jews out west!"

"Now, come here, I want to show you something," Francis said, tipping his head toward the big window in the office.

"What is it, and don't tell me ya can't stand the way the hills look stripped of all the trees. They are like grass, they actually grow back—eventually."

"What do you see down at the hitching rail?"

"My God, that's a beauty of a horse," he said as he headed for the door.

They walked down the steps and Wiesner was walking around the stallion.

"He fer sale?"

"Of course, there's only one catch."

"What's that?"

"Nobody can ride him," Francis admitted.

"We'll see about that."

In the next few minutes Wiesner had gathered five fellows who swore if it had hooves, they could ride it. They had a little paddock area where they kept the horses that pulled the logs down from where they were cut to the mill. The draft horses were tied up after they'd taken them from the paddock area. Shadow was led into the paddock, and the first of the men who wanted to ride him had put a rope halter on the horse without any problem. The saddle went on in the same manner.

"He's as gentle as a lamb," the man said as he put a foot in the stirrup. He sat up there smiling when the horse shot into the air, sunfished, twisted, then came down like a ton of bricks. The man's head snapped forward, and when Shadow bucked a couple of times, he went flying off and hit the rails—out cold. Several of the men who had thought they could ride the horse declined their turn.

"He's a sleeper, we don't want no part of him," one of the potential riders remarked.

"So, he's stud, and that's about it?" Joe Wiesner asked.

"That's right, always knew you were interested in good horse flesh. The foals of this stud will be amazing, if you can find a good mare."

"I got good brood mares, that's no problem. Let's go into the office and settle the money."

They went back up the steps as the drafts were put back in the paddock area with Shadow, who was now as calm as could be.

Joe immediately went to the safe, opened it, and pulled out a stack of bills. He counted out what he thought would be a fair price for the stud horse. It was a good offer, but as every horse trader knows, you never accept the first offer.

"I think not," Francis said, and Joe pulled a bottle from a drawer in the desk and two shot glasses. He poured and they toasted the occasion.

They haggled on like that for the better part of two

hours. By that time, the sawmill had closed and the men had already left work when Joe finally got the offer to where Francis shouldn't object, and it was settled.

"Help me take him down to the ranch and we'll have supper," Joe offered.

As they were mounting up and Francis had the lead rope on Shadow, he noticed several men sitting around in different places with rifles across their laps.

"What's the deal?" Francis asked.

"Ya saw the money I got up here. Ya just don't ride away with that kinda money in a safe."

Francis took note of the five, or was it six, positions where the men were stationed. He figured they had a routine, and this was probably always where they were. That information would be passed on to his crew.

———

Stone Child's grandfather was a patient man. He knew about rebellion, for he had rebelled just as Stone Child had rebelled. The thing about a child who rebels, the rebellion itself will usually bring the child back around, if it runs its course. So, the Chippewa Cree who had journeyed with the old medicine man trusted that Stone Child would do as he predicted. They camped in the mountains and waited undetected.

The old medicine man had been watching the young couple as they went about their work around the cabin. It seemed to the old man that they were growing closer all the while. He couldn't put his finger on it, but they stood close together when they worked together and when they did just stand around, it was always within proximity of one another.

That night, as the rest of the younger Chippewa Cree lay sleeping, the old man was visited by a Great Horned Owl. He was lying there listening to it, and it reminded him of what his father had told him about the Great Horned Owl.

"*This owl,*" his father had said to him when he was only a boy of eight summers, "*this owl can be various things. You must listen and then discern what the owl is trying to tell you each time. The rhythmic oo-oo-oo-oo of the Great Horned has told me the future at times, and at other times, it has brought me messages from the dead or great spiritual wisdom. Some even may not be birds at all. They may be relatives who have shifted from their deaths to the Great Horned and are bringing you messages from the Great Spirit.*"

The old medicine man listened intently. He lay there and the sounds of the bird swept over him as the bird might have. At one point, he felt something fly overhead. He didn't want to open his eyes because to see the Great Horned at night could be a bad omen. Their wings are fluted, and they fly with great silence, never making a noise as they glide along. In his medicine bundle, he had a grouping of feathers from the Great Horned Owl. When he needed to move without making noise, he always carried those feathers with him.

But now, it seemed this Great Horned had brought him knowledge about what was to happen. He lay there and listened, and he knew that Stone Child would be okay. The Great Horned told him that many were about to cross over into the land of the dead. Some would be kept from entering the land of the dead and would wander the earth as ghostly images seen mostly by children and old people. Others would be allowed in, but Stone Child was not to be among them. The old medicine man was greatly encouraged by this.

He hooted back to the owl. His call was recognized by the Great Horned and they had a short but informative conversation.

"Oo-oo-oo-oo! Oo-oo-oo-oo!" They called back and forth to one another. He would make a sacrifice tomorrow morning down by the creek where the Great Horned lived and thank the Great Spirit for sending him these messages.

———

Francis Grossman and Joe Wiesner rode to Joe's ranch, which was on the other side of town. Joe had purposely built the sawmill there, he liked the industry of the place and the money it brought him, but he didn't like the idea of smelling all the smoke when the wind changed directions.

Francis knew Joe's wife, Harmony, but neither of them cared for the other. Joe had hoped Francis would stay for dinner, but Harmony, in contrast to her name, was the least harmonious thing in Joe's life. She wrangled Joe into the kitchen.

"That man is not staying for supper, so don't ask," she said looking Joe right in the face.

"Who says he was gonna stay fer supper, just bought a horse from the man—a beauty, too—and thought we'd seal the deal with a drink, that's all."

"One drink, then he's out of here!" she said emphatically.

"Yeah, yeah, one and done, I promise," Joe said, and he went back into the parlor to pour the drinks.

Francis knew Harmony would never let him stay for dinner. He had known her in Kansas City when she was a soiled dove, and he never looked at her as anything else. Joe didn't have a clue, and that was fine by Francis. Besides, when he cut Joe's throat, then Harmony would be a rich widow, and what woman didn't want that?

Harmony peaked through the crack where the swinging kitchen door didn't quite close. She hated that man, Francis. There was something fundamentally wrong with the man. When she first met him in KC, he had slept and paid well for friends of hers, but she stayed shy of him. No amount of money was going to fix what was wrong with Francis Grossman. It gave her the willies just having him in her home. The sooner he was gone, the better.

The one drink was toasted and thrown back, and Francis was on his way back to town. He had a good idea of how it would all work out, and he would gather the boys and give them their instructions. First, he wanted to see who the law was and how far the law up this far in the wilderness would bother with possessing up and going after him and his gang.

He rode to the sheriff's office, turned in, and tied up his horse. It wasn't getting any cooler, and the front door was open. Two men were playing checkers under the awning out front.

"Say, fellas, is the sheriff around?"

"I'm the sheriff," an over-the-hill man said. He was dressed in overalls with no shirt on, and the badge,

Francis could see it now, was pinned through one of the suspenders of the overalls.

"I'm Francis Grossman," he said and extended his hand.

"Sheriff Holloway," the man said. He was losing at a simple game, and the other man, who didn't exactly look like a genius, was beating him badly. "What can I do ya fer?" he asked, and his checker partner, who must have been a deputy, laughed.

"That's a good'un, Holly," he said through his chuckling. This deputy was considerably older than the sheriff, and he had no upper teeth. His upper lip sucked in when he breathed, and it gave his face a cadaverous look.

"Some of my men are in town, and I've warned them I don't want any trouble. If somebody new in town gets arrested, I'd appreciate you coming and getting me at the hotel so I can take them off my payroll."

Holloway nodded his head as if he understood, then asked a stupid question. "They crooks?" he asked, and the old man with no uppers crackled again. Everybody's got to have a fan club.

"No, they're just drovers. We been driving horses to the Army and ran across a horse I thought my friend Joe Wiesner would be interested in."

"Was he?" the sheriff asked.

"What do you think?" Francis said as he pulled the sheaf of bills from his vest and showed it to the sheriff and his goofy friend.

"Wow!" the goofy friend exclaimed, "That's more money than I seen in one place in a long, long time."

"Yeah," agreed the sheriff, "I wouldn't be showing

that wad around in the saloon, ya never know what some folks will do for that much money."

"Thanks for the warning, Sheriff," Francis said. He knew exactly what some folks would do for money because he was one of some folks, and he and the Poker Brothers were going to rob Joe Wiesner that very night.

8

Uzziah and Immanuel had made their inspections of all the fortifications that Nellie and her father had made. Most of them endangered the lives of those who would carry them out, and they weren't about to let Charlie Horse, Nellie, or her pa participate in any of them. Those rifle pits in the ground, so artfully covered up, were nothing but graves where the riflemen would be shot to death once they were seen.

"What are we gonna do, partner?" Immanuel asked.

"Dern good question. Say, did ya hear those owls last night calling back and forth to one another?"

"You know me, I sleep like the dead."

"That's true."

"Were they callin' a lot?"

"Regular conversation, the way I heard it."

"Got any ideas about what they was sayin'?"

"Well, back home in Virginny, we try not to look at owls in the daytime ifn they're around, and the calls of those birds, I always thought they was a harbinger of something."

"Death mostly," Immanuel commented, "at least to the mice that are runnin' the fields at night."

"Ain't that the truth."

"So, what to do, partner, that's the question. We know this Francis is coming, but he's taking his time, trying to make us think he's forgotten all about Charlie and the girl he told them about, but we both know that ain't the case."

"I wish we had more people, that'd sure help."

"Well, we just might."

"What do ya mean?"

"Those conversatin' owls last night, did they both sound the same?" Immanuel asked.

"It were the same call, ifn that's what ya mean."

"But did one of 'em sound human?"

"Maybe?"

"Then we got help, I think," Immanuel said. "And I think it's time we go talk to 'em," he said as he walked toward his horse. Uzziah followed him but didn't have a clue what he was talking about.

———

That very night, not that far away, Francis Grossman gathered the Poker Brothers around him outside town. Someone had built a small fire and put a coffee pot on. That was good because some of them needed sobering up. Terry Pearsall was drunk, and that's all there was to it, and he was one of the better shots when he was sober.

"I want all of you to drink some coffee, as much as

you can. We're heading out early in the morning and we're going to rob an old friend of mine."

"With friends like Francis, who needs enemies," Pearsall quipped, and Francis let it slide because the man was drunk.

"Look here," Francis said as he drew in the dirt by the fire, "this is the sawmill, which is about five miles out of town and to the west. Their payroll is sitting in the safe that Joe Wiesner showed me earlier this evening. I counted six or seven guards with rifles here, here, here, here, and here," he said as he poked at the dirt, showing their positions on the dirt map.

"Like I said, there might be one more, so we got to be careful. The office and main building is here." He drew a square that showed the gang the positions of the guards relative to the office.

"Is the money just layin' 'round?" someone asked in the darkness.

"No, we're going to have to blow the safe to get at it. I bought some sticks of TNT this afternoon. We'll blow the safe with one and use the others against whatever resistance we encounter. Now, everybody get some rest. We'll spend the day up here, then ride in there tomorrow night."

———

That night, when Charlie Horse thought everybody was sleeping, he snuck to the window of Nellie's room. The window was open because it was warm that night, so he slipped through it and crawled on his belly to Nellie's bed. Her hand was hanging over the side of the bed, and he raised up and kissed it. She was sitting up quickly, and he put his hand across her mouth.

"Don't scream, it's me," he said, and he could feel her body relax in his arms.

"What are ya doin' here?"

"Ya don't want me here in bed with ya?"

"My pa would skin ya alive if he caught us, probably skin me, too. Come on, let's go outside."

They both snuck out the same window Charlie had come in and ran silently to the barn. The horses snuffled a bit when they came in, then settled back down. Horses can smell the humans they know, and when they smelled those smells, they relaxed.

The two kissed in the moonlight, which was filtering through the cracks in the barn roof that Nellie's pa had talked about fixing but never had.

Nellie had never been kissed by a man, and the way his mouth felt on hers dissolved any feelings she had about him being a bad person. Her knees went slack as he held her, and she began to have these queasy feelings in her stomach, and down from there, too. When they broke from their first kiss, she spoke.

"Don't stop," she whispered in Charlie's ear.

"I got to, or else."

"Or else what?" she asked.

"We'll make a baby," he whispered back in her ear, and then his tongue licked her ear lobe and she relaxed even more.

"You keep that sorta thing up and we'll make one right here," she said as they went back into another kiss.

There was a sound from the other side of the barn, and Nellie broke from the kiss, just knowing that they had been discovered by her pa.

"It's just me," Uzziah whispered.

"How ya know we was here?" Charlie asked.

"My partner says I can hear a fly fart," Uzziah said.

Both Nellie and Charlie giggled about that.

"Ya won't tell my pa, will ya?" Nellie sort of pleaded.

"Tell 'im what?" Uzziah asked, "Why don't ya get yerself back to bed, I need to talk to Charlie here, okay."

Nellie and Charlie kissed one more time, not like before, but like a goodbye kiss, and she ran from the barn, making no more noise than the fluted wings of the Great Horned Owl.

"What is it?" Charlie asked.

"You got people that's missin' ya?"

"What do ya mean, people?"

"Yer tribe son, all that talk about being a half-breed may fool some folks, but yer purdee somethin' I know that."

"Ya need to mind yer own business, old man," Charlie said as he bowed up a bit.

"Survival is all our business, and last night, I heard some things that might mean we ain't alone up here."

"I heard it, too," Charlie admitted.

"Then, ya know."

"Yeah, think it's my grandfather."

"Then, I think it's time we talked with him, wouldn't ya say?" Uzziah asked the boy.

The two of them rode slowly up to where they thought the Chippewa Cree were. They had a white flag out at the end of the Hawken they had recovered and they rode impossibly slow. When they finally rounded a group of trees, there sat an old man on a fine horse, and he was smiling.

"Grandfather," Charlie Horse said to him.

"Stone Child," the old man said, and they embraced sitting on their horses.

"What do the White men want with an old medicine man?" he asked.

"You know what we're waiting for, and you are here for Stone Child's protection," Uzziah said.

"Then you are smarter than you look," the old medicine man said.

"Ain't that the truth," Uzziah agreed, and all of them laughed.

"I like this one," he said as he pointed to Uzziah.

"But we can't sit here waiting for the other White men to attack us. I think you know where they are, and I would like you to take us to them."

The old medicine man sat his horse and thought for a moment.

"You wish to take the fight and not wait for the fight?" he asked.

"That's right."

"I will go with you and help Stone Child find those men, but we cannot, and will not, help you when you find them. We will wait here and protect the girl who Stone Child loves and her father."

"Sounds good, let's ride," Uzziah suggested.

————

The old medicine man talked with the other Chippewa

Cree before they left, while Uzziah went down to the porch to get Immanuel.

"Why the hell are ya wakin' me up in the middle of the night?!" Immanuel asked, not amused.

"We're gonna take the fight to the gang who bush-whacked us."

"Why didn't ya say so," Immanuel said as he pulled on his boots.

———

Meanwhile, up on the hill, Stone Child was chiding his grandfather.

"Grandfather, you have told my name to these men, why?" Charlie Horse asked.

"Because if you sing your death song and have the wrong name, the Spirit may not hear you or recognize who is singing."

"Am I going to die?" Stone Child asked.

"Someday, we will all take the road that has no return. We must always be ready, my son."

———

The old man led them to the small mill town. Even before they got there, they could see the smoke from the sawmill. As they pulled up their horses on a rise above the town, the medicine man spoke.

"They are down there with the other Whites, but they do not plan on staying."

"What will they do?" Uzziah asked the old Injun.

"That is for you to find out. Now, I go back to protect the young girl who will be Stone Child's squaw," the old medicine man said, then turned his horse and was gone.

"Guess he told you," Uzziah joked.

"But I do wish to marry her. I simply don't know how my grandfather knew?"

"Anyone with eyes, Stone Child," Immanuel said. "Anyone with eyes."

"You think her father knows?"

"No, but he looks away when you are together, he does not want to know. Now, Stone Child, you must remain here, Uzziah and I will go in and look for the men."

"But they will recognize you, and you won't know who they are!"

"Exactly, the best way to ferret out killers is to ride into their den," Uzziah said.

"I couldn't have said it better," Immanuel nodded, "but we will make it more difficult, we will ride in after the sun goes down. It will be easier at night."

———

Francis gathered what was left of the Poker Brothers into his room that night at the hotel. They stood around nervously, like schoolboys who had done something wrong.

"Well, boys, we won't spend another night in this sleepy old town," Francis announced.

There was a sigh of relief from all the boys.

"If another man says anything about me being a boy," Terry Pearsall said, "I'd have to kill him!"

"Well, just so happens, you're integral to what we're going to do. We can't have old Bill Mathers crawl into the sawmill camp without being seen, but I got an idea you'd be perfect."

"We gonna rob the payroll at the mill?" Mathers asked.

"That's exactly what we're going to do, as soon as the moon goes down."

"Can we kill the sons of bitches that'll be guardin' the place?" Manson Quills asked, a bright light of hatred shining in his eyes.

"You bet, kill them dead. There's about seven, maybe more," Francis started in as he rolled out a drawing of the setup. It was drawn well. Everyone gathered around.

———

The moon set behind the hills just as Immanuel and Uzziah rode into town. They wondered what was going to happen. As fate would have it, at that same moment, the Poker Brothers were riding out of town in the opposite direction.

The two mountain men went directly for the saloon and ordered a beer.

"That whiskey up there on them shelves sure looks invitin'," Uzziah said.

"Yeah, it do, but we got work to do, and whiskey's a poor partner," warned Immanuel.

They stood there and looked down the bar. No one standing there looked like they could give a crap that these two roughs had rode into town. Over and around at the tables, they were all more interested in their cards than anything else.

"Guess they ain't here," Uzziah said under his breath.

"My feelings exactly," Immanuel agreed. "Hey, barkeep!" he said to the man standing down at the other end of the bar. The man picked up the rag he carried habitually and walked to them.

"Another?" he questioned.

"Yeah," Uzziah said about to drain his beer, Immanuel's hand went out and stopped the guzzling of the beer.

"No, we're fine, but I got a question."

"Shoot," the barkeep said.

"There another place where gentlemen can enjoy themselves?"

"There ain't no whorehouse in town, ifn that's what ya mean? Used to be, but the preacher and his congregation ran 'em outta town."

"No, I mean another saloon?"

"Did ya see another saloon when ya rode into town?" he asked sarcastically.

"No, did I miss it?" Immanuel asked.

"Church don't want but one saloon in town, and we're it. Any other questions?"

"Yeah, where do all these men work?"

"Ya couldn't see the smoke from the sawmill. Those fires are never allowed to go out."

"That a fact?" Uzziah asked.

"Every man jack here in this town, including me, owes his livelihood to Joseph and Harmony Wiesner."

"Why's that?" Immanuel asked.

"He's the man with the vision. When he saw all them there trees strung across all them there hills and mountains, he took his money and invested in the sawmill. Everybody in here would die for old man Wiesner."

"Good to know," Uzziah said.

"Ifn ya fellas are lookin' fer work, he'll hire ya. The business is growing, in fact, tomorrow's payday and this place will be jumpin'."

It was then that the bar they were leaning against shook.

"Did ya feel that?" Uzziah asked Immanuel.

"Yeah, do ya suppose—"

There was the distant sound of what might have been thunder.

Everybody in the place stopped what they were doing and their heads turned in the direction of the sawmill.

———

Francis had thrown the first stick of dynamite, and blown the guard who was next to the office sky high. They could hear the man scream as he was torn apart by the explosion, parts of him landing hither and yon. All that was a smokescreen for Terry Pearsall, who was crawling up to the office. Everything at that moment was forgotten except for where the guards thought the next stick of TNT was going to be thrown. When one didn't come, they started shooting in the dark, missing the Poker Brothers entirely.

Unfortunately for the guards, each shot just highlighted where they were, and sticks of dynamite were thrown in their directions. Some of them hit the targets, and some of the guards got away to hide in a different location. Men were screaming bloody murder and firing randomly. So far, not a shot had been fired by Francis's men.

"I'm missin' all the fun," Pearsall whispered as he crawled up the steps, and reaching up, he opened the door while still lying on the porch. Rifle shots went right where he would have been if he'd been standing. He drew his Colt and took out the only guard in the office, who tried to scream, but his throat had been shot out. Pearsall liked his victims to suffer. The man dropped from his chair and grabbed at his throat, trying to stop the inevitable.

Pearsall got up, closed the door behind him, and swaggered into the office.

"Yer a dead man," he said, and with all the firing going on outside and the explosions that were rocking the office, Pearsall shot the man in the knees and the elbows. He had to take his hands away from his throat and grab at his other wounds, and when he did so, there was a *coup de gras* as Pearsall shot him between the eyes, "Guess ya suffered 'nuff."

He went to the safe, looked it over, then strategically placed TNT on either side of the safe. He reasoned, and he had done this before, that the explosions on either side would blast the safe door open. He lit the two sticks of TNT, then realized there wasn't any place to hide except out of the office. As he ran from the office, rifle shots ricocheted around him as he dove off the porch and into the darkness. As soon as he hit the dirt, the office was blown to smithereens. Boards and whatever else was in there were thrown into the air.

———

Francis looked on in disbelief. *What the hell*, he thought, *Pearsall had blown the place up!*

Francis nudged Manson Quills and he took off for what remained of the office as boards and splinters rained down around him. There were shots fired at him, and it gave the rest of them an opportunity to take out the last of the guards.

Manson and Pearsall made it to the safe at the same time!

"Hot damn!" Manson screamed, and that brought the rest of them, Francis, Jeremiah, and Bill Mathers, to the place where the safe had been blown open. Mathers was the last to get there, being the heaviest of them.

The money was intact, and the door of the safe was wide open.

"Good job, Pearsall," Francis said, giving him an attaboy pat on the back.

Francis held out a leather satchel and the men put the money in there, they would divide it all up when they got back to the ranch.

————

As they rode back toward the town, and the sawmill office continued to burn, putting a bright reddish glow into the night sky, they ran into Sheriff Holloway. He was sitting his horse in the middle of the road.

"Throw down yer weapons, boys!" he commanded. A big scatter gun, double-barreled and cocked, was pointed in their direction.

"You're all alone?" Francis asked.

"Hardly," he said, and torches were lit up and down the holler. There must have been fifty men.

"What the hell!" Francis said, and all the Poker Brothers took off in different directions. The scatter gun exploded both barrels, and Bill Mathers's stomach exploded and came out his back.

"Damn," he was able to say before he slid off his horse.

Two of the fifty torches were Uzziah and Immanuel. The whole town had mobilized not thirty seconds after the first explosion. This was something they had been planning on stopping ever since the sawmill was built. They divided up into different groups and took off after the remaining four badmen.

Joe Wiesner was with Uzziah and Immanuel when the sheriff's shotgun had cut the big man down.

"I saw him!" screamed Wiesner. "It was Francis Grossman!" He headed off after him. Uzziah and Immanuel followed him because they saw in the torch lights that he was the one carrying the satchel with the payroll in it.

9

Francis Grossman was not a nice man. He knew the town grew up around the sawmill, and he knew that as soon as the first explosion was heard, the whole town would be down on them. That's why he had two satchels. The one he'd put the money in and the other one, which he had in a burlap sack tied to his saddle. As soon as they rode away from the burning sawmill, he threw the satchel with the money in it behind where the great sawmill blade was used to cut the trees up. He was the last to leave, so nobody saw him do it.

No one suspected that Francis would turn right around and go back to the scene of the robbery, but that's exactly what he did. He scooped up the real satchel and he made haste for Joe Wiesner's ranch. There was a score he had to settle, and he wasn't leaving before he had done it.

———

Harmony Wiesner had heard the explosions the same as her husband, Joe.

"It's the sawmill, hon, and five will get ya ten, it's Francis Grossman who done it," he said as he gathered up his weapons and was about to run from the house.

"Be careful," Harmony said, for she knew Grossman and the way he was. At one time, he had been the most feared man in Kansas City. She feared for her husband's life but couldn't exactly tell him why.

"Oh, don't you worry 'bout me," he said. "That Francis Grossman has been itching for this for a long time." Then he ran from the house and jumped on his already saddled horse. He knew trouble was brewing when he'd seen Francis's eyes widen seeing all the money in the safe, but he never imagined he'd use dynamite.

Harmony sat in the house with all the lamps lit. She thought about how exposed she was with all that light, and she went around and blew them all out. She then sat in the dark in the parlor with a pistol cocked and in her hand. Every time she heard a noise, she would turn in the direction of it and point the pistol.

Back when Francis Grossman lived in Kansas City, he had run a soiled dove saloon and made a great deal of money. He had treated the doves like shite, and Harmony was the unofficial madam of all of them. She had sworn back then that someday she would get revenge on Francis Grossman, and maybe, just maybe, this was the time and place.

She had fallen asleep. It was stupid, but she was tired, and all the lights were out, and sitting with a loaded and cocked gun in her hand hadn't made any difference in the world. When she felt the knife at her throat, she reached for the pistol, but he had taken it from her hand.

"Nice to see you again, Harmony. I can't believe you kept the same name as back then."

"Well, it just so happens it's the name my parents gave me, and I never thought about changing it."

"Well," Francis said as he lit a lamp and kept the pistol she had had to shoot him with trained on her, "take off all your clothes, please."

"You say the worst things so properly, it just ain't right the way you talk," she said as she began peeling off all her clothes, 'til she got to her bloomers and such.

"Everything," was all he said, and she stripped the rest off, standing in her own parlor stark naked.

He tied her hands and feet to the post on the bed in the bedroom. He wanted Joe to find her in their room, raped and murdered in their bed. He just wished he could stay and see the man's face.

He pulled down his suspenders and mounted her. It always aroused him more when a woman didn't want him.

"You bastard, when Joe gets home, he's going to cut your nuts off!" she screamed in his face. He struck her hard, and a tooth flew off the bed and hit the wall.

"Son of a bitch!" she screamed.

"You never met my mother, did you?" he said as he kept getting harder as he drove into her.

Just as he was bout to finish, he drew his Bowie knife from its sheath and, placing it directly under her chin, drove it into her brain as he climaxed. He had done that before, and it made her quim tighten up just right.

He took several hundred dollars of the payroll

monies, and placed them where he'd pulled out from, just sticking out, so Joe would get the idea what she'd once done for money, then he left. The whole thing had taken maybe thirty minutes.

As he rode away, he was fairly sure he wasn't going to meet up with what remained of the Poker Brothers since sharing had never been one of his better qualities. But then again, he might need help with the posse that had sprung up out of the ground. He hadn't figured on the whole town joining up, but then again, he'd misjudged people before.

———

Immanuel was doing the best he could with the tracking when Stone Child joined them. Joe turned his gun on the Injun.

"He's with us," Uzziah said, and Joe put the gun away.

"Hey, get down here, boy, and see what ya can see!" Immanuel ordered him.

The boy Stone Child got down and examined the tracks that Francis's horse had left. They weren't easy to see in the dark, but staying with the reins in his hand and walking along, he finally announced to the others.

"Looks like he'd turned back toward the sawmill."

They rode hard for the mill, and Wiesner was mighty upset when he saw what Francis and his boys had done. Stone Child was busy figuring out what Francis had done while he was there.

"Looks like he came back to get the money, then headed east."

"He's goin' to my ranch!" Joe screamed and took off

like a shot out of hell. Immanuel, Uzziah, and Stone Child rode after him.

It took them a while to get there, and when they pulled into the ranch yard, Uzziah saw Shadow and screamed with delight. "Shadow!" he yelled and the horse whinnied and ran toward the fence. Meanwhile, Joe had run into the house, and they heard him scream, then a single gunshot.

When they got inside the ranch house, they found what Francis had done to the woman, and Joe was spread eagle beside the bed, his brains decorating the wall, the way hers decorated the headboard.

"We'd better find this hombre and put him outta our misery," Uzziah said, and the three of them ran back out to get their horses.

Uzziah saddled up Shadow and, mounting up, turned to the others.

"This horse can outrun any horse around, but I don't know where he's goin'."

"I think I know," Stone Child said as he ran his horse out a little bit, then rode back fast.

"He's goin' back toward Nellie's ranch!" he shouted, and Uzziah took off. They tried to keep up, but it was useless.

They followed as close behind as they could, and as false dawn was creeping into the east, they spotted him way ahead of them.

"That's one fast horse," Stone Child yelled over to Immanuel.

"You ain't seen the half of it. He's probably riding slower than he could, but he wants us not far behind," Immanuel explained.

Manson Quills, Terry Pearsall, and Jeremiah Bills made it back to the spot overlooking the little ranch just about the same time. Dawn was coming, and they hadn't noticed the Chippewa Cree who were hiding up further away from the ranch on the next rise.

"Where's Grossman?" Manson demanded as he looked at the other two.

"How should we know?!" Jeremiah asked.

"Do ya think he's taken all the money and run?" Terry asked.

"Again, a question we can't answer," the preacher's boy said, knowing that since original sin had entered into the world, there was just about nothing that a man wouldn't do if he took it into his heart to do it.

"We wait then," Manson said as he dismounted and went over and looked down at the little ranch.

"Let's go on down there and have our way with the girl." Pearsall suggested.

"Nah," Manson said, "ifn he shows with the monies and we're down there, he just might think we ain't deservin' of our cut."

Francis wasn't riding as fast as he probably should have, but then again, he wasn't worried about Joe Weisman. He knew Joe well enough to know that when he saw what he'd done to his wife, well, he half expected the man to do exactly as he had done. To Francis, Joe was a loser Jew. Francis was a winner Jew, and Francis judged all men of the Hebrew persuasion with the same standard. He always thought about how the Jews had been captive in Egypt, and even in Egypt, Francis knew there were winner Jews and loser Jews.

The winner Jews followed Moses out of captivity, but once they were free and Moses was up on Mount Sinai, the winner Jews gathered all the jewelry from the people and made the golden calf. No Jew in his right mind would use all the jewelry to make the calf, they'd just melt down part of it and plate the graven image. The rest of the gold went into the winner Jews' pockets. When Moses came back down finally, and destroyed the golden calf, the winner Jews gathered together the gold plate, and that, too, went in their pockets. The loser Jews were repentant, but now, they had no gold. So much for the loser Jews.

He could hear hoof beats behind him, and much to his surprise, the man they had shot before was riding the horse that couldn't be ridden. He stared back at him for some time and wished he had been able to ride that black stallion. The mountain man riding it had obviously recovered from his wounds and was now on his trail on the horse that wouldn't be ridden.

He was trying to piece together how that man had both found the horse and was on his trail. No matter how much he tried, he could not figure it out, and he was one smart Jew. It would almost have been worth it to be caught by the man just to find out his secret in riding that magnificent horse. Instead, he started shooting at him, not trying to hit the man but the horse. Any man who had a horse that valuable, and being the only one who could ride him, would not want that horse killed.

———

Uzziah saw the shots where they hit in front of the horse, and he knew this man, this low-down man who had robbed the sawmill, raped a woman, then left her there so her husband would do what Joe had done, would not stop short of killing a beautiful horse if it would keep him from being captured.

Uzziah took off for the hills because he knew that Shadow could run as fast up there as he had down in the valley. He would ride ahead of the man who had done all those evil things and surprise him in an ambush.

———

The Chippewa Cree medicine man had had a dream that night. He had seen in the dream a horse that was faster than any horse that the Great Spirit had ever made. He had also seen the younger of the two mountain men riding that horse, his hat blown back 'til the brim was pushed back by the speed of the wind. He had also seen the man who had used his wiles to take his grandson, Stone Child, away from him and place him on an evil path.

In the dream, he had feared for the fast horse because the man who was evil was trying to kill it, but the man who rode it had taken the horse out of harm's way. When he awakened, he wasn't sure what any of it meant, but he did know that the man who had done so many evil things in his life was on his way to him. His evil knew no bounds, and the old medicine man imagined he wanted to disfigure the young girl who lived with her father down at the ranch, the girl that Stone Child wanted for his woman. If it was the last thing he ever did, he would protect the girl in the ranch house, even if it meant spilling his own blood to do so.

————

Nellie and Samuel were having breakfast when Nellie let out a little yelp. She was looking toward the window, and when her father turned and looked, an old Injun riding a paint was walking his horse toward the ranch house. He had a white cloth tied to a lance and was riding with his head held high. Samuel grabbed his Greener and went out on the porch, his daughter cringing in the cabin.

"Don't come no further!" he yelled at the old Injun, who rode just a bit closer.

"What ya want?" Samuel yelled, and he certainly hoped the old man spoke English.

"Daughter," was all the old medicine man said.

"Ya want my daughter?" he asked, cocking both barrels of the Greener.

"No, daughter in trouble."

"What ya mean by that?" he asked, then realized some other Injuns could have snuck in the back way and be in the house now, taking his daughter. He uncocked the Greener and ran into the house.

"What ya doin', Pa?" Nellie asked him, his head on a swivel, looking every which way.

"Take the pistol and shoot any Injun who comes through the backdoor," he warned her, then he ran back out on the porch.

"Who are ya?" Samuel asked.

"Angel who warns of harm to daughter," the old medicine man said.

"What ya mean harm?" he asked and cocked both barrels of the Greener again.

"Only two of you, more men come, need help."

"Get off my property," he said and fired one of the barrels over the medicine man's head. Some of the buckshot tore one of his feathers from his head.

"Get ready, men come," the medicine man said.

———

Francis was almost to where he had agreed with his men that they would meet. He had obviously scared off the mountain man on the fast horse because he had been looking for him. He thought sure the mountain man would go into the hills, ride ahead of him and lay in ambush, but so far nothing. He rode harder, sorry that he had to nearly kill this horse that was his only means of escaping.

———

In the hills, Uzziah had kept pace with the man, not wanting to put Shadow in the way of danger by getting ahead of him. He saw the two of them, Immanuel and Stone Child, as they ran their horses on the trail behind the man. He rode to a rise, which was visible on the horizon, and waved his arms back and forth.

"There he is," Immanuel had said as they changed their course and went into the hills.

When they rode up on Uzziah, he had Shadow

stopped and all their horses stood there and heaved in and out.

"He was shootin' at Shadow," Uzziah explained.

"Did he get hit?" Immanuel asked.

"No, he's fine. We gotta figure out another way to the ranch, not this one," Uzziah said, then turned to Stone Child.

"Yes, there is another way into the meadow, but it might take us longer," Stone Child said.

"Then let's get goin'," Immanuel said.

They rode off together and were basically traveling a route that would bring them into the little ranch from the south.

———

"What'd the old man want, Pa?" Nellie asked.

"It was a trick, I'm sure." He said, ushering the old medicine man into the house.

"Why'd ya bring him in here?" she asked.

"He would have brought others if I let him go."

"Well, what'd he say? I couldn't hear."

"Said more men were comin' to hurt you, but don't worry, I ain't gonna let nothin' harm you."

"True, men come to hurt you, little one."

"Like I said, it's all probably a trick."

"I don't know, Pa. Charlie is half Injun, this Injun might be his people," she said, looking the old man over.

———

Terry Pearsall, Jeremiah Bills, and Manson Quills were waiting on Francis Grossman to show with the money from the sawmill payroll. All of them were getting anxious, then Jeremiah spoke.

"There's some damned Injun down by the cabin!" he whispered just loud enough for the other two to hear.

Quills and Pearsall all ran to the edge of the crest and laid down. Sure enough, there was an old Injun with slack skin sitting a horse in front of the cabin.

"What's he doin' there?" Terry asked.

"Who the hell knows, and where'd he come from?" Jeremiah asked.

"I'll take care of him," Manson said as he aimed the other Hawken they'd taken down toward the cabin.

"No, no, no," whispered Pearsall. "There might be more of 'em," he said, pulling down the barrel of the big rifle.

Manson turned on him.

"Don't ya ever do that to me again, understand?" He was hot and wanted to shoot Pearsall but didn't.

"We just need to settle down," Jeremiah said. "Francis will be here any minute—"

"How in God's name do ya know that!" Manson asked, and he didn't whisper.

"Well, I'll be damned, here he comes," Pearsall said, and when they turned, there sat Francis on a horse that looked like it had come back from the boneyard.

"What the hell took ya so long?" Manson growled.

"Nice to see you, too," Francis said as he led the horse to a nearby creek, where it started to drink.

"No!" shouted Jeremiah. "Ya want to kill the poor horse?" he asked as he pulled the horse's head away from the water. "He's gotta cool down first."

"Is that so?" Francis asked, not liking to have the reins pulled from his hand like that.

"Yeah, that's so!" Jeremiah said, not whispering.

"There's an old Injun down there talking to the pa of the girl," Manson said, pointing down toward the cabin.

Francis walked over and looked.

"Oh, really, I don't see any Indian?"

They all went to the edge of the ridge and looked. There was no one down there, not the old Injun and not the pa of the girl, no one.

"He was down there, he was!" Jeremiah swore.

"You guys are priceless, you know that?" Francis said, then added, "How'd you like your cut of the monies?"

That got everybody's mind off old Injuns and fathers of young girls as they followed Francis back to his horse, where he untied the satchel and dropped it to the ground with a thud!

10

While Francis was dividing up the payroll from the sawmill, Uzziah, Stone Child, and Immanuel had ridden around the back way. They tied up their horses in the small barn without being seen and came through the backdoor of the cabin.

Samuel turned as if he'd been snuck up on. He had the Greener still in his hands, and if it had been cocked, he would have unloaded on them since he thought it was the old man's friends.

"Whoa!" Uzziah said and held up both hands.

"Grandpa, what are ya doin' here?" Stone Child asked.

"I am here to help, Stone Child?"

"Stone Child?" Nellie asked looking at the man whom she had known as Charlie Horse.

"I knew no one had a name like Charlie Horse," her father said, smiling.

"Charlie Horse, it's not a bad name," the old medicine man said. "Who came up with it?" he asked, looking at Stone Child.

"I did," Stone Child said.

"You may have the makings of a medicine man, yet," his grandfather said.

"Stone Child?" Nellie said again, shaking her head.

"You don't like the name?" Stone Child asked.

"I'm just trying to get used to it," she said, grabbing his arm.

"What's goin' on between the two of you?" her father asked.

"We're in love," Stone Child said.

"No daughter of mine is gonna be in love with no Injun!" her father said, walking toward them holding the Greener.

Uzziah grabbed the shotgun and whisked it from Samuel's hands.

"What's the big idea?" he asked Uzziah.

"Not a good thing to hold when yer arguin' with folks," Immanuel explained for Uzziah.

Just then, a yell went up, and as they looked out from the cabin, Francis, Jeremiah, Manson, and Terry Pearsall were riding toward the cabin, firing their weapons.

Samuel grabbed his chest and slumped to the floor of the cabin.

"Pa!" Nellie yelled as she got down on the floor next to Samuel, who was losing his color fast.

Immanuel grabbed a towel off the sink in the kitchen and pushed on the wound.

"Here, Nell, press as hard as ya can on the wound," he said as shots continued to pepper the outside of the cabin and break the windows.

Uzziah had taken his Hawken and, propping it up in one of the windows, fired at one of the riders coming in toward the cabin.

A booming crash filled the interior of the cabin.

"White mountain man have cannon!" the old man said, grinning.

———

Outside, there was a yell as Manson Quills was shot off his horse and had a hole in his chest the size of a man's fist.

"What the hell!" Francis said as he wheeled his tired horse and headed back for the security of the trees. Jeremiah turned his horse and followed Francis back to the safety of cover.

Terry Pearsall rode up to where Manson was lying, dying.

"Ya come back fer me!" Manson couldn't believe his luck.

"Boss needs a horse," Terry said as he grabbed the reins of Manson's horse and took off for the hills.

"You bastard," Manson said with his last breath as Pearsall kicked his horse up and ran back to the hills, Manson's horse trailing after him.

There were three of them now. Pearsall, Francis Grossman, and the preacher's kid, Jeremiah Bills. They were sitting in the trees.

"I thought you said there was only the old man and the girl there?" Francis asked the other two.

"We told ya we saw the old Injun," Pearsall said.

"Old Injuns don't fire Hawken rifles. Give me Manson's horse," he ordered Pearsall.

"Not so fast," Terry said. "I got the horse, so what's on the horse is mine!" he shouted, referring to the saddlebags where he'd seen Manson put his cut of the sawmill payroll.

Francis shot Pearsall off his horse and, getting down, took the reins of Manson's horse and mounted up on Pearsall's horse.

Jeremiah cocked his Colt and was holding it on Francis.

"Wait, son, we'll split the payroll two ways and be rich," Francis said as he took Manson's saddlebags and held them out for Jeremiah.

Jeremiah kept his Colt trained on Francis as he reached out for the saddlebags.

"We go our separate ways, okay?" Jeremiah said.

"Of course," Francis said, and he kicked Pearsall's horse into a gallop and was gone.

Jeremiah took off in the opposite direction.

————

Back in the cabin, Samuel was bleeding to death. Immanuel had put pressure on the wound, but it was too deep and too near the man's heart. It had probably hit an artery or nicked one.

"Pa, Pa, please don't die, please!" Nellie pleaded with the man whose eyes were staring at the ceiling of his cabin as if he were seeing something besides boards.

"I...love...you," her father said to her, then his eyes glazed over, and he was dead.

"Pa! Pa! Pa!" she yelled in his face, but dead men rarely answer a roll call.

Immanuel reached over and closed the dead man's

eyes. He looked around, and all the others were against walls, waiting for the next attack. Then they heard a scream.

"They caught someone," Stone Child's grandfather said and started to walk out on the porch.

"Don't go out there," Uzziah warned him.

"No, they have fled and maybe both been caught," the old medicine man said as he walked out on the porch and signaled the hills.

Uzziah kept expecting a rifle shot to cut down the old man, but it never came. They all walked out on the porch, except Nellie, who was lying across her pa, crying.

Fairly soon, the group of Chippewa Cree rode down the hill. They had Francis Grossman's hands tied behind him and both the horses he had tried to escape on.

———

Uzziah and Immanuel had recovered two-thirds of the sawmill payroll, and they felt good about that. They didn't know what to do with Francis Grossman, who refused to talk to them. Stone Child explained in Chippewa Cree to his grandfather everything that Francis had done to the woman at the ranch and how her husband had killed himself when he found his wife.

"He should suffer the fires of hell," Uzziah said, and Immanuel shook his head in agreement.

"Onliest thing is, we won't get to watch or hear him scream," Immanuel said.

"That can be arranged," the old medicine man said, and both the mountain men looked at each other.

———

They kept Francis under guard until the next morning. He was hog-tied in the barn and still refused to make a sound.

They dug a hole for Samuel, and his daughter insisted on doing his funeral the way it would be done in Judaism. His body was undressed and placed on the big table in the cabin. She prepared a bucket with soapy water, and the body was uncovered. Uzziah had offered to help her, but she insisted on doing it herself.

They watched as she plugged the holes that were made in his body by the Hawken with corks and a kitchen towel for the exit wound. Any and all rags that had been used to stop the bleeding were gathered together. She combed his beard, and when she was done, he looked as if he just might get up and get dressed. But she had the men draw three buckets of water from the well. The water, per her instructions, was poured over his body continuously as she wiped all dirt or anything else from it. Then, she dried the body with towels. She had Stone Child take the traditional burial clothes that Samuel had in his trunks, and after pressing them, she dressed him and wrapped a sash around his waist and tied it in the form of the Hebrew letter, *shin,* which she explained to them was one of the names of God.

Uzziah had been busy in the barn making a simple pine coffin with absolutely no embellishments. A winding sheet was laid into the coffin, and a prayer shawl, which was also in the closet and which Samuel used during his prayers, was laid in the coffin and it was wrapped once around his body. One corner fringe of the prayer shawl was torn off, signifying that he no longer was responsible for having to keep the Ten Commandments.

They closed the top of the coffin by using wooden dowels and they drove those home with their hammers into the holes on the side of the coffin.

"Please forgive me if I, in any way, have shown any lack of respect in the preparation of this body for burial," Nellie said, and her countenance was amazingly serene.

The old medicine man watched all this and was very impressed.

They carried the coffin, four shouldering it out to the deep grave that Immanuel and Uzziah had dug. The medicine man was asked to be one set of shoulders, and he said he was honored to do so.

Nellie dressed very plainly and read her father's favorite Psalm from the Psalter.

"The Lord is my shepherd, I shall not want. He maketh me lie down in green pastures, He leadeth me beside the still waters, He restroreth my soul. He leadeth me in the paths of righteousness for His name's sake. Yea, though I walk through the valley of the shadow of death, I will fear no evil. For Thou art with me. Thy rod and the staff, they comfort me. Thou preparest a table before me in the presence of my enemies, my cup runneth over, surely goodness and mercy shall follow me all the days of my life, and I will dwell in the house of the Lord forever. Amen."

———

The next morning, they took Francis, who still had not spoken a word, and they tied his body together so that his legs were up under him, and his arms were tied to each shoulder. When they finished, they covered everything except his face with the skin of a freshly killed deer. It was a small bundle, considering he was a full-grown man. The man still hadn't spoken, but the expression on his face was as if he was in great pain, his body bundled up like that. They tied the bundle over a tree limb and built a small smoking fire under the bundle. It took about ten minutes before Francis started screaming.

———

Francis was still screaming when Uzziah and Immanuel went after the last of the gang, Jeremiah Bills. Stone Child, a.k.a. Charlie Horse, had said that he was a preacher's kid. He had told Stone Child that his father's church was in a small community named Auraria, where the city of Denver would eventually grow up.

They rode there and, on the way, returned the two-thirds of the payroll to the sawmill, which had been rebuilt. The men who worked there had decided they would run the sawmill as a community project and share in the profits.

When Uzziah and Immanuel rode into town, no one paid them much attention until Uzziah spoke.

"We come to return part of the stolen payroll," he said simply.

Sheriff Holloway and several of the workers from the sawmill came into the saloon.

"We hears ya got some money fer us," Sheriff Holloway said. He was still dressed in his dirty overalls and had the badge pinned to one of the straps.

Immanuel laid the saddlebags with the payroll they'd recovered on the bar. The men from the sawmill counted it. It took some time. They had lunch while they waited.

The two men who had been counting came into the café.

"There's about a third of the payroll missing," they said, looking at both the mountain men who were almost through their lunch.

"Yeah, we know," Immanuel said, "we just wanted to drop that by while we go get the rest."

By this time, Sheriff Holloway was standing there.

"Seems like they wants to abscond with part of the payroll, Sheriff," one of the men said.

"If I ain't back in a week, then come after us," Immanuel said.

"No, we's gonna keep you here while yer partner goes and gets the rest," the sheriff announced, and the two men with him grabbed Immanuel.

"It'd be a lot easier to get it with his help," Uzziah said.

"Ya got two weeks," the sheriff said as the man hauled Immanuel across the street to the little jail.

"Then what?"

"We'll hang yer partner for the killings done at the sawmill," Sheriff Holloway said as he was locking Immanuel away in a cell.

"Can we talk?" Uzziah asked.

"Sure, but make it quick, the clock is ticking," Sheriff Holloway said and walked back to the office.

Immanuel looked at Uzziah.

"I jest wish one of these times, ya'd be put some-where, so I would have to get ya back instead of the other way around."

Uzziah didn't know what to say.

"I mean, who was buried alive? Who's being put in jail? Do I look guilty or something? Why am I here and you're free?"

"I don't know the answers to those questions, but I can assure you that I will find Jeremiah and bring back the rest of the money."

"But your tracking sucks, partner, no offense."

"None taken. I'm gonna go back to Stone Child and get him to track for me. The important thing is not to worry."

———

Uzziah made it back to the little valley with the small ranch. When he got there, they were packing up. Stone Child had built a travois, and just about everything that Nellie wanted from the house was stacked on it and tied down.

"Where ya goin'?" Uzziah asked, sitting his horse.

"This place reminds Nell too much of her pa. We're going to eastern Montana territory to live with the Chippewa Cree."

"Is this what you want, Nellie?" Uzziah asked.

She didn't speak but shook her head in agreement.

"But yer pa is buried here."

"That's one of the reasons my grandfather invited us to live with him and the tribe. He was so impressed by what Nellie did for her pa once he was dead. He said hardly any of his people pay that much attention to the dead, and he hopes she can revive the burial practices of the Cree."

"It's gonna be cold in the winter and hot in the summer, I can tell ya that," Uzziah said, then added, "I need yer help finding Jeremiah, the preacher's boy."

"I haven't got time for that right now," Stone Child said.

"Immanuel got exactly ten days afore they hang him in that little town."

"He didn't steal the payroll. It was Francis and the rest of the Poker Brothers."

"I know that, you know that, but it don't make no difference to this Sheriff Holloway. He'll swing Immanuel out over eternity as sure as I'm sittin' my favorite horse, Shadow."

Stone Child went over to Nellie, who leaned down from the horse she was on while he whispered in her ear.

"Okay, we'll go with ya, but after that, ya have to help me and Nellie get to the tribe in eastern Montana, deal?"

"Deal," Uzziah said, and the two men shook hands.

———

Due to the travois and Nellie being in tow, they traveled slowly. Stone Child remembered that Jeremiah had told him that his pa had a church somewhere in the Colorado territory. That didn't help that much, but when it was explained that two rivers found their confluence there, Uzziah thought he knew the place. He'd never been there himself, but Immanuel had said someday that confluence would be a big town.

They took off immediately. It took them several days, and Uzziah realized, since he'd been making marks on a sheet of paper, that one week was gone. All he had left to find the preacher's boy was seven days. Then, he had to make allowances for getting back to the sawmill town with the money. All he could think was it was a good thing that he rode a fast horse.

They rode into the town and saw the church. Many people were talking about it because the son of the preacher had returned, a regular prodigal story. He'd gone out into the world and made his fortune, and he'd return to invest in his father's ministry, help them rebuild the church. In fact, this Sunday, which was the day after tomorrow, at the service, the boy would be honored and the monies accepted. His preacher pa liked formal occasions, and this was going to mark the beginnings of their ministries together.

"What's the boy look like?" Uzziah asked the patron at the bar he'd been talking to.

"Well, he's a young one, like I said, yella hair, and fit as a fiddle. We're all pretty happy things turned out the way they did."

"Yeah, sounds too good to be true," Uzziah said and finished the beer.

He wasn't quite sure what to do, so the three of them camped outside of town in a swale where they wouldn't be seen. Cottonwood trees lined this little creek, and the mornings were cold, but the trees kept their smoke from alerting the town they were out there. Obviously, they couldn't both go ask the boy for the money back, so Uzziah decided he'd do the asking.

Maybe the boy hadn't seen him properly when they attacked, maybe he'd actually turn out to be a Christian and do the right thing. Uzziah wasn't sure what to do, but he would ride into town today, it was a Saturday, and ask the boy, Jeremiah, for the money, and see what happened.

————

Uzziah tied Shadow loosely to the hitching rail, down at the end, in case he had to make a fast exit. There was no telling what was going to happen. He'd play it by ear and see.

The boy was standing at the bar and fellas were buying him drinks. It was like he was a war hero or something. Uzziah was about to rain on that parade.

He bellied up to the bar, and having gained back most of his weight, he really did belly up. The boy was next to him, explaining how he'd gotten the money. It was a fairly fanciful story, and Uzziah didn't pay much attention to it. When the boy finished with the tale, the older gentlemen there bought him drinks and then wandered off. He was left with the boy right beside him. It was then that the boy turned to him. He was fairly drunk, not exactly a good beginning for a new preacher.

"Ya been here the whole time?" he asked Uzziah.

"Just got into town," Uzziah said, and the boy took off on the tale of how he got the money, although this time, it was a different story. Uzziah figured he didn't want to mess up a good story by sticking to any facts.

"What'd ya think of that, old man?" the boy asked, and he was really in his cups now, Uzziah having bought him a couple whiskeys as he lay like a rug.

"I ain't much older than yer pa, ya call him old man?"

"Ya not my pa?"

"Not really, but I do know how ya got yer monies."

"Of course, ya know, I just told ya," the boy said, scoffing and throwing back the last whiskey Uzziah had bought him. "I gotta get home and prepare my sermon fer Sunday," he said and started to walk away. Uzziah grabbed him by the shirt. He turned and looked at the mountain man as if he'd just seen him.

"That's ill-gotten gains," Uzziah said, not wanting to outright accuse the boy.

"What in God's name are ya talking about?" The boy shook Uzziah's hand off his shirt.

"That's the sawmill payroll, well, a third of it anyway," Uzziah said just loud enough for the boy to hear.

There was a moment when Uzziah thought the boy was going to draw on him, a big mistake. First of all, he was drunk, second, Uzziah already had the Hawken loaded, leaning up against the bar between them. All he had to do was lean it more in the boy's direction and pull the trigger.

"Don't," was all Uzziah whispered.

"Don't what?"

"Get yerself kilt."

"Are ya threatening me?" the boy said, his voice low and menacing. "Why all I have to do is tell these people yer here to take my money, which is dedicated to the church, and you'll be hanging from the closest tree in town," he said with a smirk on his face.

"Ya done robbed me once, son," Uzziah started in. "Remember when you and yer gang jumped them two mountain men and took everything they had after shooting me and clubbing my partner?"

It was then that the boy recognized Uzziah. Well, it was about time.

"Just hand over the monies and I'll leave town, nothing else said," Uzziah offered.

"This man's trying to rob me of the monies fer the church!" the boy yelled as he backed away from Uzziah.

There was a commotion as several men gathered around the boy. Uzziah was walking slowly from the saloon.

"Hey you, wait!" someone yelled, and Uzziah heard a pistol cock.

When he went through the plate-glass window, no one was more surprised than he was. He rolled to his feet and, jumping over the hitching rail from the board-walk, he was on Shadow and riding out of town as fast as that stallion could carry him. Amazing what a big man can do when he has to!

He heard shots and felt a couple go past him and the horse. He looked back to see if Shadow had been hit, and he hadn't. When he looked up, he saw several horses coming after him. Well, it was only a matter of time, wasn't it?

He rode away from the kids, and by the afternoon, Shadow wasn't even winded, and the last of those who had chased after him had given up, except for one man, who must have had the next to fastest horse in town. Uzziah rode for the hills, and when he got up there, he stashed Shadow behind some boulders, took out the Hawken, and lying on a rock, he leveled it on the hombre. He didn't know this man from Adam, but what was he to do?

———

The man was a good half mile away when his hat was torn off his head, and then he heard the shot. What the hell! This guy was firing from an incredible distance and shooting a man's hat off without shooting out his brains was a trick indeed, especially from that distance. He wheeled his horse to a stop and raised his hand palm toward the hills where the man had shot from.

———

Uzziah knew exactly what that meant. He was being thanked for not killing the man. He rode back to the confluence town and left Uzziah in the hills.

11

He rode around the little confluence town and back to where Stone Child and Nellie were camped.

"What happened?" Stone Child asked.

"I tried to get the boy interested in something besides what he's doing, but no luck."

"What are ya gonna do?" Nellie asked Uzziah. He turned to her.

"Go to plan B, I guess?" Uzziah said as he poured himself a cup of coffee off the fire.

"What's plan B?" Stone Child asked.

Uzziah fixed them all dinner—beans, bacon, and biscuits. His Dutch oven had been with all the other stuff that Francis Grossman had taken from him. They listened as he told them what he wanted to happen when plan B was put into effect.

———

It was Sunday. The church was packed, which was perfect. Jeremiah Bills sat up front on the dais with his pa, Pastor Bills. The older man was quite proud that his only son had returned home with enough money to completely restore the church, and now, it seemed he had decided that he would follow his pa into the ministry. Things were especially looking up. Pastor Bills had thanked God that night and each night since his son had returned for the boy's return and his newfound wealth. He had a few niggling questions that kept being asked in his heart, but this money would save the church, which was about to fold. Pastor Bills's wife was buried in the cemetery out behind the church, and he now figured he would be too, eventually.

The sack of money that the boy had stolen along with Francis Grossman was still in the satchel that Grossman had put it in. It was lying center stage right up at the foot of the pulpit. The service began. They opened with an old hymn, and the voices of the congregation sounded great since it had swollen to such a size. The boy, Jeremiah Bills, was leading the singing. He had a fine voice, and since he was the hero of the hour, everyone loved to see him up there singing and waving his arm around like he was directing music.

As the song was about to end, he saw a woman, a girl, really, get up and open the double doors of the church. Well, maybe it was a little hot in there. He'd have to thank the girl later. She was pretty and maybe—

He never got to finish his last thought as there was a dull smacking sound as .54 caliber bullet entered his brain just above his eyes and threw a lot of brains all over the cross which was hanging at the back of the dais, just as the booming sound of the Hawken was heard.

Pandemonium broke out in that little church. Nellie ran up to the body, looking like she was going to help the stricken man, but instead, she grabbed the satchel and ran for the side door of the church. People were crawling under the pews as two more shots entered the church graciously through the open doors. Those shots were for crowd control, and control the crowd they did.

When Nellie ran from the pastor's office, she threw the satchel to Stone Child, who was holding the reins on her horse. Uzziah had taken the travois and hooked it up to Shadow and was quite a distance away, reloading.

The kids rode fast out of town, but neither of their horses were Shadow. A posse was hastily gathered, then another man was wounded with the Hawken. He was shot in the arm, and no one could tell where the shots were coming from. Uzziah had decided to stop the posse before it began and give the kids a chance to get away.

They were supposed to meet up at the creek about five miles out of town, but Uzziah waited 'til dark and nothing. Stone Child had absconded with the money, and he and Nellie were nowhere to be seen.

"Well, by God, by gum, by Jove!" Uzziah said to himself, wondering when he'd stop being hornswoggled by others.

———

By the time he made it to the sawmill town, he had one day left. Gallows had been built by Sheriff Holloway, and the entire town seemed to be celebrating. *Well, hangings do bring out the best and most festive in people,* Uzziah thought.

He waited 'til dark, and it seemed the town was wasting no time, they were all getting drunk at the only saloon in town. Uzziah snuck around to the back of the jail and, looking through the bars, saw his partner curled up on the cot in the cell. He was about to speak when a man with a minister's collar appeared at the bars and spoke.

"Can I offer ya God's salvation?" the man asked.

Immanuel stirred on the cot, rolled over, and put his hands behind his head.

"What's that padre?"

"Oh, I ain't Catholic, are ya Catholic?"

"Yep, I thought ya'd come to offer me last rites."

"No, no, no, can't do that, don't know how, but Jesus saves, ya know?"

"Yeah, and Moses invests!" Immanuel said with a smile.

"I don't understand?" the preacher said.

"It don't matter," Immanuel said, "Just run along, if ya will."

The preacher looked sad but left Immanuel lying on the cot.

"Pssst!" Uzziah made a noise at the cell's window.

Immanuel got up and walked to the window. Uzziah was slinking down below it, in case Sheriff Holloway showed himself.

"Ya comin' to the winder makes me think ya ain't got good news," Immanuel said with a bit of resignation.

"It ain't," Uzziah said.

"Couldn't find the money, huh?"

"No, I found it, I mean *we* found it all right."

"So, where is it?"

"Stone Child took it."

"Damned Injun!" Immanuel swore under his breath.

"Are ya ready to get back to the mountains and our cabins?"

"Duh!"

"Take this here rope and tie it right around the bars."

"Criminals again, I guess," Immanuel said as he was reaching for the rope.

"Whatcha doin' there?" It was Sheriff Holloway.

"Nothin'," Immanuel said as he draped both hands through the bars.

"Yer hands are free, ain't they?" the sheriff quipped.

"Freehanded as hell," Immanuel said, never turning around.

"Hope yer ready to die, come tomorrow noon, we havin' ourselves a hangin'," the sheriff said, laughed once, then walked back to his office.

Uzziah lifted the hemp rope to his partner, who took it and tied it tight around the bars.

Uzziah got Shadow and tied the other end of the rope to the horn of his saddle after making sure the cinch was tight. He looked back to Immanuel, who had his hat on now. Well, at least he was ready to go. Then, there was a stroke of luck. The town had bought some fireworks and they were being launched, from all places, the gallows. They were exploding overhead, and when Shadow pulled the window right out of the cell, Immanuel jumped through the hole and no one was the wiser.

They rode double down to the hostlers, where Immanuel went in and got his horse.

"Thought they was gonna hang ya, tomarrie?" the old man said.

"Nah, my partner brought back the money, everything's okay now."

"Well, guess you'll be wantin' these," the old man said as he held out Immanuel's Hawken, his gun belt, and pistol. "Want me to saddle the horse fer ya?"

"Sure, old man, that'd be great," Immanuel said and handed him a coin.

———

They rode from town with the glow of multicolored fireworks going off in the sky. Once out of the town limits, they kicked it up and headed for Stone Child's village. They traveled throughout the night but were still a few days from the eastern Montana territory. That night, while they set up camp, Immanuel went out and shot them an antelope. The pronghorn was good eating and Uzziah had made his famous Dutch oven biscuits, and they got full. Coffee was made, and Uzziah brought out a couple of pieces of crushed cake that he'd put in his saddlebags.

"Damn partner, are ya gonna purpose?" Immanuel said, eating the cake right off the paper it was stuck to.

Uzziah told him the entire story. How he'd tried not to hurt the boy, Jeremiah, but had killed him in the end.

"Good, no-good bastard deserved to die. So, ya say Nellie was the one who got the satchel back, huh?"

"Yep, why else would they have disappeared if they hadn't got the money?"

"Money'll do strange things to folks when they get it. Kids probably didn't even think of dealing ya dirt 'til they actually had it. Money may not be the root of all evil, but the love of it surely is!"

"I guess," Uzziah said, cleaning the tin plates in the little stream that ran by where they were camped.

"Hey, don't be too hard on 'em. We'll find the village and get the money back, then take it down to the sawmill town and let every man jack know we ain't thieves."

"At this point, we should just keep it," Uzziah said, half joking.

"I know that's a joke. Because we done kilt an officer of the law back in St. Louis, and that was a cause of she whose name we do not speak. I ain't plannin' on burnin' no more bridges, are you?"

They smoked. Uzziah didn't have to answer a question that Immanuel already knew the answer to. These two mountain men were the most honest mountain men they knew, so no questions asked. The monies would be returned, and that was that.

————

That night, while they were sleeping, they heard a bunch of buffalo wander by not too far away. They were both grateful that the herd hadn't stampeded. They had done that dance once before.

In the early morning light, as Uzziah fixed breakfast, Immanuel walked off from the camp. When he came back, beans, bacon, and left-over biscuits were eaten.

The second day out, they were riding along a trail

and one rider was coming toward them. It wasn't that usual to run across people, everyone was going somewhere. As they got closer, all three men waved. The wave was created—Immanuel had read once—in medieval times, when knights came across each other on the roads, and the open hand was simply the fact that they weren't holding a weapon. But that didn't mean they couldn't draw one fairly quickly.

"Good day to ya," Immanuel said.

"Good day," the man said and looked both the mountain men over. He wasn't dressed as a mountain man would be, so they figured he must live around here close.

"We're lookin' fer a bunch of Chippewa Cree. Do you know of a settlement of them nearby?" Uzziah asked.

"I ain't been there, but the word is on the eastern side of the Montana territory, there's a good-size village of them. Why ya lookin'?"

Uzziah looked at Immanuel, who answered that question.

"A while back, we got acquainted with a young Chippewa named Stone Child, and he's got something of ours."

"They're a fairly peaceful lot, I've heard," the man injected.

"Yeah, that's our experience, too," Uzziah said, then added, "What's yer interest in our interest, young son?"

In a saloon, people could ask you all sorts of questions, but out here on the plains, it was rather unusual for a man to ask other men questions about what they were doing.

"Just making conversation, that's all," he said and looked at them nervously.

Both mountain men shook their heads and looked at each other as if they were passing some unspoken message between them.

"Well, thanks for the information about the Chippewa Cree. We'll be on our way, friend," Immanuel said as he put his hand on the Hawken and moved it closer to the direction the stranger was sitting on his horse. Immanuel had noticed earlier that the man wore his holster low on his leg, and it was tied down with wang leather.

The man went for his holster, but Immanuel's Hawken exploded as it lay across his lap and the man looked down at the hole that the .54 caliber had made in his chest.

"What the—" he said as he slid off his skittish horse and dust rose up and settled down on his body.

"Immanuel?!?" Uzziah yelled.

Immanuel got off his horse and looked through the dying man's pockets. He was rewarded when he hit the inside left pocket of the man's vest. He pulled a folded dodger from it and opened it. He looked at it, then showed his partner. It was a good likeness of Immanuel, and said there was a $500 reward for him, alive or dead. It listed his crimes as stealing the sawmill payroll and escaping from jail.

"What the hell?" Uzziah said, then went on, "How did they get dodgers out so fast on you?"

"Guess they really want that money, old son," Immanuel said as he squatted down beside the dying man.

"Where'd ya get the dodger?" he asked the man who was bleeding profusely.

"Bastard," was all he said as his eyes became fixated, and the last shuddering breath left his body.

———

When they saw the Chippewa Cree village, they had in tow the horse of the bounty hunter and whatever else they could use. No sense in leaving guns, ammunition, knives, or anything. Uzziah had found some good bacon and flour in the man's saddlebags.

"Well, there's the village. Let's go get ourselves the man who left you in jail," Uzziah said.

They rode in quiet and easy. The boys taking care of the horses who were grazing along a small creek saw them first, and one of them ran off to alert the village while the other stayed to watch the horses. Immanuel had taken the saddle off the bounty hunter's horse, and he released him to the boy watching the Chippewa Cree horses. The horse ran off and joined the other horses, and the boy waved his thanks.

Once they were in the village, they were surrounded by kids, squaws, and old women. The braves were off somewhere. An old man came from a tent that had been alerted to their presence by one of the small boys.

"It's you," he said, and both Uzziah and Immanuel realized it was Stone Child's grandfather, the medicine man.

"Good to see you," Uzziah said. "How is your health?"

"I walk with a bit of a limp, but other than that,

good medicine keeps me well," the old medicine man said.

All right, they had made the usual obligatory niceness which was required within native societies. Perhaps they would smoke the pipe, but Immanuel wasn't sure.

"Your grandson—"

"Stone Child?"

"Yes."

"He was here, but he left right afterward," the old medicine man said.

"Why did he leave?" Uzziah asked.

"It was the girl, the one whose father was killed, and she did so much preparation for his grave. I liked her and thought she would make my grandson, Stone Child, a good squaw, but he was anxious when he arrived, and I put it off to their travels and the new squaw, actually his second squaw."

"But?" Immanuel asked.

"It was his soul. He had done something bad."

"You mean something else bad. He was one of the men who ambushed us back a few months ago," Uzziah said and showed the bullet wound in his shoulder by pulling back his shirt.

"I thought I could change him, but sometimes, the young, they have their own notions which do not run within the tribe."

"Where'd he go?"

"The girl was talking all the time about her departed father."

Uzziah and Immanuel looked at each other and realized they were chasing someone who was running and not settling down.

"Please stay tonight, let us feed you and show you hospitality after everything my grandson has done to you both."

————

They stayed that evening. They were asked to smoke with the medicine man, and his granddaughters treated both Uzziah and Immanuel with a great deal of respect. After they ate, and neither of them was sure what they'd eaten, but it was good, Stone Child's grandfather sat next to them.

"Will you take one of my granddaughters for a wife?"

Both mountain men looked at each other. It had been a while since either had had a woman, but buying into the whole marriage thing was a bit much.

"I'm gonna pass," Uzziah said, knowing that Immanuel would do the same.

"Which ones are your granddaughters?" Immanuel asked, and Uzziah was truly shocked. They had a Chippewa Cree to find and money to recover if they were to get the dodgers off Immanuel. What was the older mountain man thinking?

"This one here," he said as he touched the young girl on the shoulder. She was sitting beside him. "And that one there," he added as he motioned to a particularly beautiful young woman in a brown deerskin dress. She had full bosoms and shapely legs, and her hair was like a raven's. The high cheekbones on her face highlighted her brown, brown eyes, which were big and expressive.

"You like her, I can tell," the old medicine man said,

and he motioned again to the young girl and she came over, where she sat beside Immanuel.

She sat there the rest of the night, and she and Immanuel smiled at each other and he signed to her things, which Uzziah wasn't sure what they meant. Finally, as the evening was winding down, she looked at him, walked to a nearby teepee, went in, and before she closed the flap, smiled one last time.

"I can't believe this," Uzziah said.

"What, that I'd be so lucky?"

"No, that you'd be so foolish. She's young enough to be your daughter."

"But she isn't."

"She's a child, Immanuel."

"Yeah, but their culture has these young girls having papooses long before most White women even consider marriage."

"So, you're going to marry her?"

"Her grandfather said I could try her out. She had been married, but a fever took her husband, or so he said. If I like her, she's mine, if not, she'll stay here."

"Well, that's awfully convenient."

"Look, partner, you went off with that pistol of a girl, and when ya came back, I thought ya'd jumped the broom or whatever, then neither of us even had a taste. At least this way, if she goes with us, she'll do a lot of chores around the cabins, have a good place to raise babies, and she'll sleep with you too," he said, smiling at what was becoming his best friend.

"Like the one whose name we cannot repeat?"

"Maybe, but at least this way, we know it'll just be the two of us, so if she gets pregnant, we'll know one of us is the father."

"This is wrong," Uzziah said and seemed to mean it.

"Well, ifn she was enticing you, I wonder how ya'd feel about it?" he said as he got up. "I'll see ya in the morning, then we'll take off after Stone Child. What do ya say?"

"Fine," Uzziah gave up and turned away from his friend.

12

As it turned out, Immanuel liked her a lot. Evidently, her last husband, the one who had been taken by the supposed fever, had taught her a few things, and those few things were enough for Immanuel. The next morning, he told the medicine man that he'd like to take her with them. They held an innocuous ceremony beside a fire that morning, and the medicine man threw smoke around them, everyone smoked the red clay pipe, and then a leather thong was tied around their joining hands, and it was done.

Her name was Flying Feathers, and with that name, they expected that she would be difficult at some point, but they could hardly tell she was there. The amazing thing was her late husband had evidently been one hell of a tracker because she was able to—over rocks, granite, through streams, and on other various hard-to-track places—follow Stone Child's tracks like she had made them herself.

Not surprisingly, those tracks led them back to the

little meadow where the Jewish father of Nellie had been buried with such ceremony. They sat up on the hill, much the same way that Charlie Horse, a.k.a. Stone Child, had sat up there and spied on Nellie and her pa before this whole thing started.

Flying Feathers made the most smokeless fire that either of the two mountain men had ever seen. She cooked, cleaned, slept with Immanuel, tried to get in Uzziah's bedroll, but he politely refused, and she went back to Immanuel's bedroll. The next morning, as they were eating and she was gathering wood, Immanuel laughed.

Uzziah looked at his partner.

"You want to know what's so funny, huh?"

"Well, yeah."

"She wants to sleep with you, and your refusal made her wonder if you were berdache?"

"What the hell does that mean?"

"Queer, basically."

"I hope you told her."

"That you were?"

"No, that I'm being polite. She's your wife."

"She wouldn't understand that. If you don't sleep with her, she will assume you are berdache."

"Well, I'm not."

"I know, but...she don't."

"Fine, I'll sleep with her to settle things."

"If she makes you the offer again, that is," Immanuel said, smiling.

"Can't I just go to her tonight?"

"That'd be three of us in my bedroll, then she would know that you were berdache!"

"Oh, for goodness' sake!" Uzziah said, he was so frustrated.

It was about then that she returned with an armful of wood, which she gently deposited near the fire, not wanting to make a lot of noise since they had snuck up on the man and his squaw below them.

————

That night, as the sun was setting behind them, the two mountain men crawled up to the crest of the hill and looked down.

"Look, that's a new wagon by the barn, and five will get you ten, that there's new furniture in the cabin," Immanuel said.

"Ya think Nellie gone along with the theft?" Uzziah asked.

"Uh-huh," Immanuel said. "After all, she was the one who took it from the front of the church with the dead body of Jeremiah lying there."

They spent the better part of that night trying to decide exactly what to do. Those kids had taken the money, but Uzziah felt that they wouldn't actually kill the two of them to keep it.

"Are you willing to risk your life and my life for such a gamble?"

"That's a damned good question, which I am at this juncture unable to answer," Uzziah said.

The whole time, Flying Feathers was listening. While she was cooking, while they were eating, she always ate after them, and they had a habit now of leaving her some of the best portions of whatever they were eating. Just because she let them go first didn't mean that they couldn't be gentlemen about it.

They all went to their bedrolls without deciding much. In the middle of the night, Uzziah thought he was having a dream, something kept poking at him. When he opened his eyes, it was Flying Feathers, and she was naked and trying to get into his bedroll. He opened it for her, and she snuggled next to him. His only thought was, *I guess she don't think I'm a berdache anymore.*

When he awakened in the morning it was almost like it was a dream. Flying Feathers had their breakfast ready, and Immanuel was still asleep. And yet, he had the sweetest memory of her climbing on top of him and riding him like he was some unbroke pony, 'til he exploded inside her. One of these days, that woman was going to get pregnant!

They got up, ate. Immanuel didn't look at Uzziah funny, and he wondered if even he knew what she had done. He was beginning to think that that squaw was acting on her own and that no matter how much control they thought they had over her, she was actually a free agent. He had no idea how close he was to the truth.

"Are we goin' to git the money this morning?" Immanuel asked his partner.

"Yep, we is," was all Uzziah said.

They had had a good breakfast. Sometime that morning, before either of them had awakened, she had killed a rabbit. There wasn't a shot, so she must have got it in a snare. He didn't even know or remember if he had seen her set a snare. Didn't matter, the rabbit was delicious, and Uzziah guessed she didn't want her men to go out in battle without full and grateful stomachs.

Once on their horses, Flying Feathers stood beside Immanuel's horse and looked up to him. He signed down to her what they were getting ready to do. Uzziah's signing was something to be desired, but he understood that Immanuel had told her he loved her, and that if they didn't come back for her, to steal his horse from those below and go back to her tribe. The woman took the news as if Immanuel was giving her a grocery list. She didn't blink an eye. Got to love them sentimental Indians.

They decided they would take the long way around and come in from behind the cabin. The very route that Stone Child had shown them before. That way, those two thieves wouldn't think there was someone on the ridge to the east.

They rode in real quiet-like with a white flag, an old bandana Uzziah had had for ages. It had seen better days. It was more like a tattered rag than a parley flag.

They had to give the kids credit, Stone Child walked out with his rifle in hand, a new one, both mountain men realized it was a Henry 44 caliber, and mighty pretty. He held it down, both hands on it, it could be jerked up real fast, and both men noticed it was cocked.

"What you two old men want?" Stone Child asked, as if he didn't know.

"Well, hello to you, too," Uzziah said, then added, "You remember my partner here, the one they kept in the jail and were going to hang ifn I didn't bring back the rest of the sawmill payroll?"

"Hey, Immanuel, glad ya didn't swing," Stone Child said, but his voice was still hard as nails.

"That makes two of us," Immanuel admitted.

253

"Guess ya came fer the monies, didn't ya?" Stone Child said, his hands moving ever so slightly on the Henry.

Well, they had their Hawkens loaded and cocked and lying across their laps on their horse. Uzziah simply hoped that if the kid started shooting, he'd miss Shadow.

"Yes, as a matter of fact, we did," Uzziah said, and Shadow, sensing some evil intent, began to dance around a bit.

"Ya'd better calm that horse down, or I'll kill 'im."

"I think he knows that, that's why he restless," Uzziah said as he pulled on the reins and got the horse under control.

"Well, we done spent a passel of it," the boy said and then, by God, he grinned.

"We know, done seen yer new wagon, a beaut, and that there rifle, I'm fairly sure they ain't givin' them away," Immanuel said.

"Ya can't get us both, and you'll die tryin'," Uzziah grunted, getting ready for a firefight always made his stomach hard.

"Yeah, well, ifn it comes down to that, guess who's got a bead on one of you from the house?"

They hadn't figured on Nellie getting into the fight, but money does strange and amazing things to people, especially once they start spending it. Doesn't matter if it's theirs or not, the spending of it convinces them it couldn't be anybody else's. There was only one person that both men had met who knew just what money was, and they couldn't say her name anymore.

"Well, kid," Immanuel started in, "it was nice knowing ya."

Just as all hell and all firing was about to break loose, a scream came from the cabin, and Flying Feathers, her hair all wild and untamed, came running out of the back of the cabin with a Bowie knife at the throat of Nellie. She had pressed so hard with it that Nellie's neck was already starting to bleed a bit. Immanuel saw his knife and wondered at her ability to get it off him without him knowing, must have been when she said her goodbyes?

"What the—"

Flying Feathers started squawking in Chippewa Cree, and it must not have been very nice talk because Stone Child's eyes grew big, then he lowered his weapon. Flying Feathers yelled some more in Cree, and he dropped it to the ground and, of all things, started crying.

Uzziah and Immanuel just looked at each other as if they were witnessing Moses parting the Red Sea.

"What in heaven's name?" Uzziah said, but Immanuel was silent. His Cree had improved a bit since he'd begun shagging Flying Feathers, and Uzziah figured he'd picked up on most of what was being yelled at the boy.

The Chippewa Cree woman let Nellie go, and she ran into Stone Child's arms, and they both wept.

———

They, the three of them, Uzziah, Immanuel, and Flying Feathers, were headed back to the small sawmill town. They had found what was left of the money that Stone Child and Nellie had robbed. They'd go in hot, with weapons drawn, and talk with Sheriff Holloway. No way in hell were they going to let that bibbed-overall sheriff get the drop on them again. That outfit of his was just a disguise. Under those overalls sat the cold-blooded heart of a gunslinger.

Uzziah rode up close to where Immanuel was riding, and Flying Feathers was way behind, singing some Chippewa Cree song.

"What's she singin' back there?" Uzziah asked.

"Far as I can understand, it's her death song."

"I didn't think squaws had death songs?"

"Well, she does."

"Guess we figured out why she's called what she's called," Uzziah said, chuckling, and his belly was moving with the humor.

"Uh-huh," was all Immanuel said.

"What was she screaming at Stone Child back at the ranch? Could ya understand any of it?"

"Uh-huh."

"You aren't gonna tell me?"

"You really wanna know?"

Uzziah just gave Immanuel the death stare.

"Okay, okay, don't get your union suit in a wad. Guess who her husband was afore he ran off and joined the Poker Brother's Gang?"

"Nah!"

"Yep!"

"You mean?"

"Yep."

"Well, blessed mother of Jesus, who'd have thunk it?"

"Yeah, she was tellin' him not only would she cut his new squaw's throat, but she would nut him afterward."

"No!"

"Yes!"

"Damn, she done earned that name, didn't she?'

"Rightly so. Now, are ya sad I took a bride?"

"Not anymore," Uzziah said, looking back at her still singing her death song.

"And she ain't bad in the sack, is she partner?"

Uzziah's head whipped around so fast, he almost gave himself a neck ache.

———

Immanuel figured that Flying Feathers was singing her death song because she had a notion that riding in without all the money might cause them some problems. They rode in in the middle of the day. The sun was at its zenith, and it was hot as hell. The sawmill was going full steam, they could see the smoke roiling from the chimneys. They rode right up to Sheriff Holloway's office. He was sitting out there playing checkers with the same old man, like the first time.

"Sheriff," Immanuel said, and the two men looked up and it took a moment before the sheriff spoke.

"Ya got some nerve, I can sure say that."

Immanuel threw the satchel down at the sheriff's feet. He didn't move. He saw they had come loaded for bear, and Uzziah's head was on a swivel, looking for the sheriff's backup.

"They're all at the mill," was all he said, and Uzziah concentrated on the two checker players.

"It ain't all there," Immanuel admitted.

"But mostly?" the sheriff asked.

"Mostly."

"Ya owe me for the back wall of that cell."

"I'd take it outta the satchel, we ain't big on easy-flowing cash," Immanuel said.

"And you's the one that done it, ain't ya?" he asked, looking at Uzziah.

"Yep."

"Had to kill a bounty hunter who was lookin' fer me."

"That a fact?"

"Yes, and ifn those dodgers are pulled and ya don't issue anymore on me or my partner here, we'll be even. But if they ain't pulled, and any new ones are circulated about Uzziah and him breaking me outta jail, well, we'll come back and murder the whole town," Immanuel said, and even Uzziah believed him!

"Done," the sheriff said as he looked at the checkerboard and did a triple jump on the old man.

"Sonny beach!" the old man sorta swore.

"Didn't see that comin', did ya?" Sheriff Holliday said to the old man.

"Well?" Immanuel was being emphatic, and when he got that way, he was liable to shoot somebody.

"No more dodgers, on neither of ya, say, who's the purty squaw?" the sheriff asked, licking his lips.

"She's about to be the death of you," Uzziah said, swinging his Hawken toward the sheriff.

"Didn't mean no disrespect, none atall. Will ya join me in the saloon fer a drink?"

"Hell no!" both mountain men said at the same time, and all four men laughed heartedly, but Flying Feathers kept her hand wrapped around a pistol Immanuel had given her.

EPILOGUE

They left the little sawmill town and didn't look back. Well, Uzziah checked their backtrail a couple of times and was rewarded with a smile from Flying Feathers. She was no longer singing her death song and seemed right at peace with herself.

It took them nearly a week to get back to the cabins, and every night, Flying Feathers cooked, cleaned, and gave them what each man wanted and deserved. It was almost like they were reunited with she whose name they could not speak.

When they rounded the last boulders and the cabins came into view, well, you'd have thought Flying Feathers was looking at the Taj Mahal. She screamed something in Cree so loud that, later, Uzziah admitted to Immanuel that he had tinkled himself a bit.

She worked all through the next few days, cleaning, fixing, and being the woman she wanted to be.

That third night she was so tired, she fell asleep as she was cooking supper. Immanuel carried her into the cabin with the pot-bellied stove, she liked that one the best, and he laid her down on the buffalo robes. He kissed her on the top of her head and walked back out, where Uzziah was finishing up dinner.

"We done good, partner," Immanuel said, glad that it seemed that they just might be back to where life would take on a rhythm that they both loved.

"We did, that's a fer sure," Uzziah said, spooning the concoction of deer meat and some wild vegetables that Flying Feathers had found onto two tin plates. He handed one plate to Immanuel and spooned a healthy portion from his plate into his mouth.

"Hot, hot, hot!" Uzziah said as he tried to jostle the stew around in his mouth to keep from burning him so bad.

Immanuel smiled and waited for the stew to cool. It smelled wonderful, and all was right with the world.

A LOOK AT BOOK THREE: TROUBLE WITH THE LAW

A UZZIAH MOUNTAIN MAN WESTERN DOUBLE

The law is closing in. The mountains may no longer be enough.

Uzziah O'Bannon and Immanuel Jones return in another double-barreled tale of survival, grit, and hard-earned brotherhood on the unforgiving American frontier. Their names are known. Their freedom is wanted. And the men hunting them are better equipped, better funded, and won't stop until they're in chains—or buried.

When word reaches Uzziah that his mother is deathly ill, the two mountain men make a risky journey east, only to land in the crosshairs of the Pinkertons—and a cavalry force fifty men strong. The reunion turns to retreat, the family homestead to a battlefield, and safety becomes just another dream left behind.

But trouble doesn't end when they return to the Rockies. A run-in with the legendary Jim Beckwourth and his four Crow wives draws them into another mess—with dead men, vengeful twins, and fresh victims left in the gang's wake. Wounded, hunted, and in over their heads, Uzziah and Immanuel must rely on the only thing they've ever been able to count on: *each other*.

This two-book bundle includes the fifth and sixth novels in the Uzziah Mountain Man series.

AVAILABLE OCTOBER 2025

ABOUT THE AUTHORS

He was good looking and could sell ice to eskimos. But ... writing asked something else from him. He would have to corral his interest in being free. Writing would take him to a place where he was tamed, but also able to actually tell a story.

After the first two weeks at the Yale School of Drama, he called the head of the playwriting department, Milan Stitt and told him he was quitting. Milan invited him to lunch at a nearby Mexican restaurant in New Haven. He told the man who had had plays on Broadway that he wanted to be a free writer. Milan smiled, then explained the way to freedom was always through discipline.

Something in him clicked and it all began to make sense.

Three years later, when he received his MFA in playwriting, he received the much coveted Cole Porter Prize for Excellence in Writing.

Enter a woman, years later, when the first 'J' in J.J. Bonham, Jack Bonham, had written thirty screenplays in 7 years and had one optioned which looked like it actually might be done.

Unlike Milan Stitt, this woman had no plays on Broadway, but was a divorced mother of four grown children. She loved soaps, and was an ardent watcher of the same. In the years of her devotion to watching she developed an uncanny ability to discern plot and analyze character. Uncanny, really better than any of his teachers at Yale.

They, Jack & Judy, the other 'J' in J.J. Bonham, married in Buffalo Springs, Colorado. While teaching elementary school in Denver they read the same novella and looking up and into each other's eyes, realizing something. They could do that.

Thirteen years later they had written nearly 200 novels. Westerns mostly because that was who they were – a misplaced couple from the 19th Century who saw life in a western justice sort of way. They danced in Virgina City, Montana. Dances from a different time and place, but still their time and place.

Now, they live in the Bitterroot Valley on five acres and looking out the office window as he puts this together for them, he can see the thunderstorm marching across the Sapphire Mountains. Earlier, sitting on the porch, she had said something about the crack of lightning years before as they said vows of love in Buffalo Springs. He remembered.

www.ingramcontent.com/pod-product-compliance
Lightning Source LLC
Chambersburg PA
CBHW010825250626
47169CB00010B/2965